WILD DREAMS

Wilder Irish, book twelve

MARI CARR

This book is dedicated to Nan, my partner at work and in crime for twenty-nine years. Be sure to save a spot for me on your back porch for wine and plotting after your retirement!

PROLOGUE

Patrick Collins slowly rocked back and forth as his youngest grandson, Oliver, nestled in his lap. He was spending the night at his son Sean's home, babysitting. Sean was currently at the hospital with his spouses, Lauren and Chad. Sadly, Lauren, who had been ten weeks pregnant, had suffered a miscarriage earlier in the evening.

Patrick had driven to their house the moment Sean called to ask if he could stay with Oliver. His chest grew tight as he considered the tension in his typically affable, happy son's voice. This wasn't Lauren's first miscarriage. In truth, it was her sixth, each loss driving the sadness that seemed to be his daughter-in-law's constant companion even deeper.

Lauren had dreamed of a large family, a houseful of kids. After she'd first married Sean and Chad, she'd told her husbands countless times she wanted to break Patrick and Sunday's record of seven children.

She hadn't made that joke in years.

Patrick knew Sean was worried about Lauren, and not just her physical health but her emotional state as well. This evening when she'd gotten in the car, she looked like a ghost of her former self, an empty shell. She hadn't shed a tear. Patrick suspected it was because she'd cried every single one of them out over the past decade. His heart ached for her, for Sean, for Chad.

Sean had been fearful of another miscarriage ever since Lauren told him she was pregnant again. She'd suffered four miscarriages before Oliver came along. And since his birth...two more. Sean had confided in Patrick just last week that this was it. He simply couldn't watch his wife's heart break again, couldn't suffer the pain of losing another child.

They called Oliver their miracle baby and no little boy was more doted on, more adored.

Oliver had just turned five and usually he was a rambunctious ball of energy. Patrick often compared him to a bull in a china shop, something he'd often said of Oliver's father when he was growing up as well. The boy took after Sean in terms of stature and disposition. He was a full head taller than the other kids in his kindergarten class, his strength was off the charts, and he was never without a huge grin on his face.

Patrick's daughter, Riley, had given him the nickname Bam Bam a couple years earlier, likening him to *The Flintstones'* character, after Oliver, only three at the time, had managed to dismantle the stone border she'd placed around her herb garden.

There was none of that energy present in Oliver tonight. While he didn't know where his parents had gone or why, Oliver clearly sensed something terribly wrong had happened.

The two of them had claimed this rocking chair on the front porch after Sean and Chad got Lauren to the car, the three of them driving away, and they'd remained just like this for the better part of an hour.

Patrick thought perhaps Oliver had been tired, but the young boy hadn't fallen asleep. Instead, he sat quietly on his lap, looking out across the yard.

"Would you like to go inside and watch TV, lad? Or maybe have some ice cream?" Sean told Patrick they'd just finished dinner when Lauren had felt the sharp pains, then noticed the blood. Mercifully, Oliver hadn't seen any of that.

Oliver shook his head. "I'm not hungry."

That response told Patrick everything he needed to know. Oliver might not understand what was going on, but if the boy was turning down dessert, it was obvious he was scared and sad.

Patrick decided it was time to distract the boy from his heavy thoughts.

"Have I ever told you what your name means, Ollie?" Patrick asked.

Oliver twisted in his lap to look at him, shaking his head. "What it means?"

Patrick loved learning about the history of names, the meanings, the symbolism. He'd taken to telling each of his twelve grandchildren about their names. Some, like Padraig, loved hearing the stories tied to past namesakes, while others, like Colm, were less impressed by the game. Granted, Padraig had the fascinating story of St. Patrick driving the snakes from Ireland to entertain him, while the best he'd had to offer Colm was the symbol of the dove.

"Every name has a meaning. And in your case, it has three."

Oliver grinned, clearly excited by this discovery. "What does it mean?"

"Well, some people say Oliver is derived from the olive tree. Have you ever heard the expression extending an olive branch?"

Oliver shook his head, his brow furrowed in confusion. "What's an olive branch?"

"It's a limb, a twig, from a tree." Patrick pointed to the large maple in the front yard, then to the ground below it. "See that stick over there?"

Oliver nodded.

"That's a branch from that tree."

"Why would somebody want a stick?" Oliver crinkled his nose, unimpressed by the gift.

Patrick chuckled. "Well, in this case, the olive branch isn't actually there. It's more of a symbol."

Oliver tilted his head and Patrick hastened to continue his explanation, lest he lose the boy's interest.

"If someone extends an olive branch, it means they are offering a promise not to fight. It's meant as a symbol of peace and friendship."

"Like the way I gave Billy half my peanut butter in jelly after I accidentally knocked him down at recess?"

Patrick grinned at the way Oliver insisted on calling his favorite sandwich peanut butter *in* jelly, despite how many times his parents had explained it was peanut butter *and* jelly. Of course, Oliver also referred to his second favorite sandwich as a girl cheese rather than grilled. The silly names amused Patrick to no end.

"I think that's a perfect example of what it means to extend an olive branch. So Oliver means peaceful." In Patrick's mind, it was a perfect representation of his grandson. While Oliver sometimes struggled with his size and his strength, he genuinely hated to ever see anyone hurt or sad, and he didn't doubt his grandson truly had given away half his favorite lunch to make amends.

"What else does it mean?" It was clear from Oliver's tone he was less than impressed with being peaceful. And Patrick was reminded of Colm's outright disdain over being compared to a dove.

"Oh, you'll like the second meaning. It's a good one. According to the Norse, Oliver means affectionate."

"What's that mean?"

"It means you are very loving, that you like kisses and cuddles and hugs and tickles." Patrick backed his description up with an example of each definition, grinning widely when Oliver giggled as he tickled him.

"I like that one."

Patrick had suspected he would. Oliver loved nothing more than to curl up on Patrick's lap for a cuddle during story time.

And he practically bowled Patrick over every time he saw him, running to him for a huge hug.

Patrick ruffled Oliver's hair. "I knew you would. But...I've saved the best for last."

Oliver's eyes widened with curiosity.

"The Germans claim that Oliver represents an elf army."

Oliver laughed loudly, his delight almost tangible. "That's silly, Pop Pop."

"Yes, but just think of all the fun you could have with an elf army. So many magical opportunities."

That idea sparked Oliver's imagination, just as Patrick knew it would, and for the next hour, the two of them remained in the rocking chair, creating their own elf army stories, each fictional adventure more outlandish than the next, until Oliver fell asleep in his arms.

Patrick remained there, enjoying the closeness and refusing to relinquish it. His heart panged as he realized there would most likely be no more newborn grandbabies to hold. Oliver, the youngest, would be the last. He placed a kiss on the young boy's head, looking down at his sweet, innocent face as he slept.

Now, as always—whenever he was with one of his grandchildren—he thought of Sunday, and for a moment, he allowed himself to pretend she was sitting right there beside him on the porch.

"Ah, lass," he whispered, closing his eyes. "I miss you so."

A slight breeze ruffled his hair, feeling so much like her fingers, caressing him. And then he imagined her voice, whispering back, "I'm right here."

$\maltese$ I $\maltese$

Four years ago...

"How was your date?"

Oliver jerked at the unexpected voice, unaware of Gavin's presence until he spoke. "Hey, man. Didn't see you there. Why are you sitting in the dark?"

Gavin Hawke, Oliver's foster brother, was sacked out on the couch in the living room of their parents' house. His folks were out of town for the weekend on an impromptu trip to New York. Oliver's fathers, Chad and Sean, had surprised his mother with tickets to see *Hamilton* on Broadway.

"I was watching a movie. It ended and I'd just turned the TV off when I heard your car pull into the driveway. Thought I'd see how your date went."

Oliver walked into the room, turning on a lamp before dropping down next to Gavin. Gavin had come to live with his family when they were both fifteen, and while the first year had been a pretty rough adjustment for them both, over the past five years, Gavin had become his best friend, the two of them as close as true brothers.

Oliver's eyes lit up when they landed on a pizza box on the coffee table, and he leaned forward to flip open the lid.

Hot damn. Jackpot. Two pieces left.

Oliver grabbed both, flipping one over on top of the other to make a meat lover's sandwich, and took a big bite.

"Didn't you just go out to dinner?" Gavin asked.

Oliver grimaced. "Mmm-hmm," he muttered, his mouth full of food.

"Must be that wooden leg your Pop Pop swears you have."

Oliver swallowed and shook his head. "Not exactly."

Gavin reached for a beer bottle on the end table and took the last swig.

That was when Oliver noticed there were several empties on the floor. "Private party?" Though they weren't quite twenty-one yet, they'd been sneaking beers from their dads for a couple of years. Their dads pretended not to notice because they never took it too far. Given the fact Sean and Chad had been best friends their entire lives, and Sean had grown up above the pub, Oliver was pretty sure they'd done the same thing when they were younger.

Gavin lifted one shoulder casually. "Rare for me to get the place all to myself. Thought I'd take advantage of it, try out the bachelor concept. Watched some porn, drank a few beers, ordered a large pizza, farted, scratched my balls, and burped at will."

Oliver laughed before shoveling in another bite of pizza. "Wow. Best night ever. I should have stayed here with you."

"Guess that answers my question about how the date went."

Oliver reached for a napkin, wiping pepperoni grease off his chin. "The best two words I can think of to describe Vivian are 'high' and 'maintenance.'"

"That's not good," Gavin muttered.

"Tell me about it. She insisted we try some trendy new restaurant downtown that all her girlfriends have been raving about. Cost me sixty bucks a plate for five bites of food. She kept going on and on about how great it was, even suggested we go back again next weekend."

"Okay. So not a wooden leg. You're hungry."

Oliver tore off a large chunk of the crust. "Fucking starving."

"Not like it was your first date with her. You know what she's like."

"Yeah. Even so. I'm breaking it off. Would have done it tonight, but...fuck...I was too hungry to even figure out what to say."

Gavin snorted in response, then set his beer bottle down with more force than necessary.

For the first time since he'd walked in, Oliver noticed Gavin hadn't smiled. Not once. Which was unusual for Gavin.

"You okay?" Oliver asked.

Gavin nodded, but a tightness around his eyes and tension in his jaw proved he wasn't.

"Anything you want to talk about?"

Gavin started to shake his head—Oliver noticed the slight movement—but he stopped himself. Then his best friend turned on the couch to face him more fully. "How come you never go out with guys?"

Oliver blinked, completely blindsided by the question. "What?"

"The day I told you I was gay, you said you were bi."

Oliver had suspected Gavin's sexuality right from the beginning, but his foster brother had grown up with an abusive mother, one who'd beaten him down year after year until Gavin had learned the best defense was a good offense.

As such, his thoughts and feelings had been locked down tighter than a drum, and it had taken years of living with not one but two psychologists—Chad and Lauren—before Gavin felt safe enough to slowly reveal pieces of himself to his foster family. Oliver didn't bother pretending they didn't still have a long way to go.

Gavin had come out to him just six months earlier. Not that he'd needed to actually say the words. Oliver had seen through what Gavin had called "a night out with the guys" when they were in high school. Obviously, "night out" was code for a date, and they were always with just one guy, most of whom were very openly gay.

Oliver had never admitted to knowing because he knew Gavin would tell him when he was ready, and he'd learned that pushing for answers only caused his foster brother to shut down and pull back even more.

Oliver could still recall how happy he'd been when Gavin finally opened up to him. And he'd been glad for the chance to open up as well, revealing he was bi, and that he dreamed of a threesome marriage just like his parents had.

While society might not consider Sean, Chad, and Lauren's relationship normal, to Oliver, they had everything anyone could ever want.

And he wanted the same.

Desperately.

What Oliver *hadn't* said to him that night— mainly because it would freak his foster brother out—was that he hoped his future would include Gavin.

With Gavin, he'd learned more was accomplished with baby steps. The fact it had taken his foster brother five years to come out of the closet certainly proved that.

Gavin had laughed about his future plans, calling them "Ollie's wild dreams," and life had continued the same as always. The only difference was Gavin started calling his dates what they were—dates—and he'd begun to share some details about his sex life with Oliver.

"I *am* bi," Oliver said at last, confused by Gavin's comment.

Gavin's scowl grew darker and Oliver tried to understand what he was saying wrong, why Gavin was so annoyed.

"Right."

The dismissive tone proved that Gavin thought he was lying...and it pissed Oliver off. "What's your problem?"

Gavin schooled his features as he shook his head and stood up. "Nothing. I don't have a problem."

Now, as always, Gavin planned to walk away. It was a standard Gavin Hawke move. Hit and run. His foster brother didn't do fights, didn't lose his temper. Instead, he'd take a quick jab and walk away. Considering Gavin had spent the first decade and a half of his life as a punching bag for his mother and her insane rages, Oliver could understand that.

Sort of.

And sometimes, Oliver let him get away with it, if he thought the fight wasn't worth it or if it felt like something that would blow over.

Other times—like now—he dug in.

He followed Gavin upstairs, dogging his heels. "What the fuck, Gavin? What kind of game are you playing?"

Gavin turned when he reached the door to his bedroom. And while Oliver's temper was tweaked, Gavin was cool as a cucumber.

Which, of course, pissed Oliver off more.

"I'm not playing a game, Ollie. I'm saying you're not bi."

"And you think you can judge who I am, what I feel, better than me? Fuck you."

"Have you ever kissed a guy? Given a blowjob? Fucked one?" Gavin's tone was almost weary.

Oliver narrowed his eyes. "Seriously? You know I haven't."

Gavin snorted, acting as if that somehow proved what he was saying.

Oliver couldn't let it stand. He wouldn't. "You want to know why I haven't?"

Gavin frowned. "Because you're straight."

Oliver lifted his eyes toward the sky. "Jesus Christ, you're thick. I haven't fucked a guy, or kissed one, or blown one because I don't want anyone but *you*."

It wasn't often that he and Gavin weren't on the same page—after so many years of close friendship, sometimes it felt like they shared a hive mind—but it was obvious they were on opposite poles right now.

Had Gavin really never sensed Oliver's attraction to him? There had been times—brief moments—when he'd truly thought he'd given his feelings for his best friend away. Obviously he'd been wrong, a better poker player than he'd thought.

"What the fuck are you talking about?" Gavin asked, his tone rife with shock.

"I've always known you were gay. Knew it five minutes after you moved in here."

"Why didn't you say anything?"

Oliver shrugged. "I knew you'd tell me when you were ready."

"You expect me to believe you've been saving yourself for me? All these years?" Gavin asked.

"I wasn't saving myself. At least not on purpose. The truth is, I wasn't sure about my own sexual preferences until…"

"Until?" Gavin prompted.

Oliver debated whether or not he should come clean about this particular little secret, and then decided it was time to put his cards on the table. "I saw you with Billy Newcome. That night we all went camping right after graduation. I woke up in the middle of the night, needed to take a piss. Saw the two of you in the woods. He was bent over and you were fucking him."

"That was almost two years ago."

"I know. Jesus. I knew I should leave, but I couldn't walk away, Gavin. Couldn't stop looking at…"

"At what?"

"You. I'd have given a million dollars to switch places with Billy that night."

"Why didn't you say something?"

Oliver had wrestled with that same question ever since that night, but there wasn't a simple answer. "We're best friends, Gavin. Brothers. Besides, you were doing a lot of," he finger-quoted, "'nights out' with Billy, and I was dating Lori Matthews."

"Both of those relationships ended a year ago."

"So you admit it was a relationship," Oliver joked.

"Ollie," Gavin pressed.

"Fine," Oliver said with a rueful grin. "I don't know why, okay? Come on, man. It's not like it would have been easy to cross that line. We still live at home with our folks."

He expected Gavin to laugh, but he didn't. Instead, he shook his head, not in denial, but as if he was trying to puzzle out something he'd missed. "You want me?"

Oliver took a deep breath. There was a time for words and there was a time for action.

This happened to be the latter.

He and Gavin were about the same height, both of them well over six feet, so it was the simplest thing in the world to reach out, grab his best friend's face, and kiss him. He ran his fingers through Gavin's dark brown hair, gripping it in his fist. Gavin had started wearing it a bit longer since they'd graduated from high school, something Oliver teased him about, calling him a hippie.

Gavin's shock was brief, and the second he opened his mouth and started kissing Oliver back, it confirmed everything Oliver had always known.

He and Gavin were meant to be. The two of them would find a woman, marry her, have kids, raise them together, and his dreams for the future wouldn't seem so wild. They'd be perfect... just like what his parents shared.

He pressed Gavin against the closed door to his bedroom, grinding his hips closer, needing him to feel his hard-on, to understand exactly how much he wanted him.

They parted briefly, trying to draw in enough air so they could go back in. They were both breathing rapidly, but Oliver couldn't resist this. Not a second longer. He resumed the kiss, tasting the beer on his best friend's breath.

Gavin reached for the knob and opened the door to his bedroom. The two of them backed inside, Oliver kicking it closed behind them. Neither of them was willing to break this kiss, as too many pent-up desires exploded free.

Gavin reached behind his neck and tugged his T-shirt off

one-handed as Oliver stepped back to watch. They'd seen each other naked at least a thousand times. They were brothers. They shared a bathroom and clothes.

Oliver also knew he was the *only* person who'd ever seen Gavin shirtless. Not even their parents had, and though Gavin had told them he had some scars, he'd seriously downplayed them.

Oliver couldn't begin to imagine what their dads would do if they saw how bad the damage truly was. And their mom would definitely fall apart. Gavin had said as much to Oliver, begging him to keep quiet. Oliver had reluctantly gone along with it, so Gavin had successfully hidden his chest—wearing T-shirts even when they went swimming, claiming he sunburned easily—to protect *their parents* from pain that *he'd* suffered. It was so typically Gavin, and one of the reasons Oliver loved him so much.

Now—as always—Oliver's heart lurched painfully as he looked at the evidence of too many fucking years of abuse. He felt as if he could map the scars on Gavin's chest, his back, his upper arms, all left there by a cruel woman who knew how to wound where no one would see.

He recalled the first time he'd seen Gavin without a shirt. His foster brother had been living with them for just over a year.

Gavin had seen the inside of too many foster homes, too many group homes, and he'd shown up here at fifteen with a chip the size of Texas on his shoulder, certain this house would be like all the others—temporary.

That first year had been the longest of Oliver's life, and he was ashamed now to think of the number of times he'd begged his parents to send Gavin away. His parents had refused time after time, insisting that Gavin needed to be with them.

When he looked back, Oliver realized getting sent away had been Gavin's intention as well. He'd been attempting to beat all of them to the punch, and his cruel, cutting comments to them, his bad attitude, his failing grades, the things he stole or destroyed, were all his way of hurting Oliver and his parents before they could hurt *him*.

Oliver thought back to the night he'd busted into Gavin's room after discovering the hundred bucks he'd been saving all summer—earned by mowing lawns in the neighborhood—was gone. He'd been fully ready to kick the shit out of Gavin until he gave it back.

He'd caught Gavin unaware, in the middle of changing his clothes, his back turned to the door. The fist he'd drawn as he'd stormed into the room vanished when he saw the round, puckered scars left from cigarette burns and the thin white lines covering his back, drawn from what Gavin later admitted had been broken beer bottles.

And while his anger had vanished, Gavin's had erupted.

It was the first and last time he'd ever seen his foster brother lose his temper.

He'd shoved Oliver hard, screaming at him to get the fuck out. Oliver had held his ground, asking, "Who the fuck did that?" over and over as Gavin kept shoving him away. For every step he was pushed back, Oliver closed the distance, moving closer, demanding again, "Who the *fuck* did that?" until all the rage, all the heat, seeped out of Gavin, and he dropped down onto his bed.

Oliver had never seen a sixteen-year-old boy look so exhausted, so utterly defeated.

He'd sat down next to him, and while Gavin would only say it had been his mother, the walls between them began to crumble that night. They'd remained there for hours, sitting side by side, as silent tears streamed down Gavin's cheeks. Hell, Oliver had shed more than a few tears of his own that night.

Oliver reached out now and, for the first time ever, ran his fingers over Gavin's chest, touching more burns, his heart aching as he thought of the little boy who'd been terrorized by the woman who was supposed to love him, take care of him.

Gavin gripped Oliver's hand, flattening it against his pec,

letting him feel the racing of his heart. Their gazes locked. Mom insisted no one who didn't know them would realize the two of them weren't related by blood, given their similar features—both had brown hair and dark brown eyes—and builds.

Unlike Oliver, who'd shaved just before his date, Gavin was sporting a sexy five-o'clock shadow that showcased his chiseled jaw. Oliver longed to lean forward and nip it with his teeth.

"Take off your shirt, Ollie."

Oliver loosened the tie he'd donned for his shitty date, and then unbuttoned his shirt. Like him, Gavin didn't seem capable of keeping his hands to himself. He ran his hand over Oliver's bare chest, then gripped his waist, pulling him back to continue the kiss.

Oliver grasped Gavin's upper arms, digging his fingers into the tattooed muscles there, keeping him close when it felt like he might pull away. Gavin had started getting tattoos the second he'd turned eighteen, his attempt at mitigating the damage, hiding the scars.

"Ollie," Gavin murmured, shaking off his grip. "Pants, now. This is gonna take all night if I have to tell you what to do step-by-step."

Oliver grinned. "Smart-ass. Apparently I have something to prove to you." Oliver reached for the waistband of Gavin's lounge pants, pulling them down. He wasted no time taking Gavin's cock in his hand, stroking it with a firm grip.

"Fuck," Gavin whispered as Oliver dropped to his knees in front of him.

Oliver gave him a wink, then took the head of his dick into his mouth. While he'd never given a blowjob, Oliver wasn't a stranger to receiving them. He knew what he liked, and even what he'd always wished for from women who—lacking a penis—never seemed to fully understand exactly how to suck a guy's dick.

Oliver gave Gavin the kind of blowjob he'd always wanted, and given the way Gavin's fingers gripped his hair, the way he thrust his hips back and forth, the way he said Oliver's name over and over, it was apparent he was hitting the mark.

"Goddammit, Ollie. It's too good. You need to slow down or—"

Oliver wasn't fucking slowing down. He took Gavin deeper, swallowing his dick, as he reached lower to fondle his balls, then stroke his perineum.

Gavin cursed as he came in Oliver's mouth. "Motherfucker! Jesus Christ. Ollie. God. *Dammit.*"

Oliver held him in his mouth a few moments more, even as Gavin's cock softened. Releasing him with a pop, he rose slowly, pulling Gavin to him for a long, heated, passionate kiss.

"Lube's in the drawer," Gavin said, turning toward his night-stand. He grabbed it and a condom, handing both to Oliver, who tossed them onto the bed so he could take off the rest of his clothing.

"Bend over the edge of the mattress," Oliver said, stroking Gavin's ass as his friend assumed the position.

Everything between them felt so natural, so right. While it was his first time—*their* first time—there was no hesitance, no reticence, no second-guessing.

They were meant to be together.

Oliver squeezed some lube on Gavin's anus, working it in slowly with one finger, then two. He was in no hurry. If he could make this night last a year, he'd do it.

Gavin wasn't feeling quite as patient. "Jesus, Ollie. Put the condom on and get on with it. I want you inside me."

Oliver chuckled but gave in. Maybe his self-control wasn't that great either. Once he'd covered his dick—with the condom and more lube—he placed it at the entrance to Gavin's ass.

Gripping Gavin's hips, he pressed forward slowly, steadily.

Holy shit.

This felt like heaven...and for a moment, he was actually light-headed. "Jesus," he whispered. He'd never experienced anything like this. Gavin's ass was so tight, gripping his cock like a glove.

Gavin dropped to his elbows, groaning with pleasure, overwhelmed as well.

Once Oliver was seated to the hilt, Gavin lifted his head and looked at him over his shoulder. "I want it hard. If you hold back, I'll know it."

Oliver nodded, words beyond him right now. He withdrew until just the head of his cock remained lodged within and then he gave in to his primal urges, taking everything he wanted, then grabbing more. He fucked with wild, reckless abandon, confident in the fact that Gavin wanted the same.

They clawed at each other like beasts, pounding together in a way that should have hurt but instead felt like fucking paradise. Gavin shoved backwards, meeting every single one of Oliver's thrusts.

It was brutal, ruthless, even violent.

Oliver came first, his body jerking, as if he'd been electrocuted.

Gavin, lost in his own need, didn't seem to even realize he'd come as he kept shoving back, kept fucking himself on Oliver's dick.

Oliver's fingers tightened as he tried to stop the motion. He couldn't fucking take any more. It was too good...too much.

He reached around Gavin's waist and gripped his cock, jerking him roughly until Gavin exploded, his come splashing over the bedspread.

Neither of them moved for several minutes, still connected as they gasped for breath. When he felt his strength begin to return, Oliver pulled away, locking his knees in an attempt to remain upright. Removing the condom, he tossed it in the trash can.

Gavin pushed up as well, twisting to sit on the edge of the bed. He glanced over his shoulder at the stained bedspread and smiled. "Oops."

"Come on." Oliver reached out, pulling Gavin up to stand next to him. "We'll sleep in my bed."

They crossed the hallway to Oliver's room together, pulled back the sheets, and crawled in.

Gavin shifted closer, kissing him once more, their gentlest, calmest kiss of the night.

"Okay. So maybe you *are* bi," Gavin joked.

Oliver erupted in laughter, the two of them shaking the bed for several minutes, neither capable of pulling themselves together without cracking up again.

Finally, they managed to settle down, both lying on their backs, staring at the ceiling. Oliver reached out and grasped Gavin's hand.

"We're on our way," Oliver said, his heart too full to hold in his feelings.

Gavin glanced in his direction, his eyes curious. "On our way?"

"To our future. Now all we have to do is find our bride and we'll be there."

"Bride?" Gavin's sudden stillness should have been a warning sign, but Oliver was flying too high from everything they'd just shared. So he foolishly kept talking, pounding the nails into his coffin, one after the other.

"Yeah. I mean, it's definitely not Vivian, but that doesn't mean the perfect woman isn't out there for us. We just have to find her, and then...then we can have a life just like our parents. We'll have a houseful of kids and dogs and cats. We'll take over the construction company when Justin and Killian and Dad retire. The three of us will grow old together, sitting on the front porch, surrounded by grandkids. I'm going to tell all of them the meaning of their names, just like Pop Pop does. I can see it all so clearly, Gavin. Our future begins tonight. It's ours for the taking —and I can't wait."

"Ollie." If Gavin's expression hadn't told Oliver he'd just fucked up, his tone certainly did.

"What's wrong?"

"I don't want that. You gotta know I don't want that."

"What do you mean?"

"I know what kind of relationship your parents have."

"*Our* parents," Oliver corrected, something he did constantly. Even after five years, Gavin couldn't quite accept or believe that he was truly a part of this family.

Gavin ignored him. "I can't do—"

"Of course you can," Oliver insisted. "Is this because of your mom? This isn't you worrying that you're like her or anything, is it? Because come on, you know—"

Gavin shook his head. "I know I'm not like my mother. I'd never hurt a child. Ever. That doesn't mean I want one." Gavin stood up, and Oliver sensed he was trying to pull away, seeking to put distance between them. After everything they'd just shared, Oliver hated it, but he resisted the need to pull Gavin back into the bed, knowing his foster brother didn't respond well to pressure, to being forced into anything.

"You'd be a great dad," Oliver offered lamely.

"Jesus, Ollie. You don't get it. You didn't grow up like I did. You've spent twenty years as a Collins and it's skewed your vision, blinded you to just how fucked-up and shitty the world really is. I'm not bringing a kid into it. Not ever."

"Gavin—" Oliver started.

"No. Stop and listen to me. And then *think*. Think really hard. Do you think you could be happy in a relationship with just the two of us? You and me. No kids. No wife."

Oliver didn't reply. He couldn't. "I love you, Gavin."

Gavin gave him a sad smile. "I love you too, but that doesn't answer my question."

"I..." Oliver dug deep, tried to find the words, but he couldn't say them. Couldn't lie to his best friend.

"Yeah. That's what I thought."

Oliver felt the first spark of panic, aware of just how badly he'd misread everything.

"It's okay," Gavin continued, the sad look in his eyes, breaking Oliver's heart. "It's okay, man. You just forgot one thing."

"What?"

"Unlike you, I'm *not* bi. I'm gay. I could never be part of a relationship like the one Sean, Chad, and Lauren share. Never. And it wouldn't work for you any other way."

"Maybe..." Oliver started, but he stopped short because he knew Gavin was right. Oliver longed for a threesome, a true marriage of three hearts. Him as the lynchpin, with a boyfriend in one room and a girlfriend in the other, wouldn't work. And he wanted kids, wanted to be a dad more than anything in the world.

Gavin sighed, then he bent down and kissed Oliver. This wasn't a prelude to more. This kiss was a goodbye. Pure and simple.

"I'm glad I was your first," Gavin said. "You're always going to be my brother, my best friend. Tonight didn't change that."

Oliver swallowed hard, trying to dislodge the lump in his throat, wishing he could find something—anything—to say.

"Night." Gavin walked back across the hall to his bedroom.

Oliver sat in his bed for hours, staring at the closed door to Gavin's room, fighting for an answer. A way.

Until a few hours ago, Oliver would have sworn there was nothing he wouldn't do, wouldn't sacrifice, for his foster brother.

But it turned out, there was one thing he *couldn't* give up.

His wild dreams.

❧ 2 ❧

Present Day

"Dammit, Sunnie. You need to slow down. The tree looks ridiculous with so many ornaments at the bottom and not enough at the top." Oliver took the three ornaments Sunnie had grabbed to put on the Christmas tree.

Sunnie put her hands on her hips but didn't try to take the ornaments back. "So sue me. I can't help it if I'm height-challenged. Besides, if you guys would spend more time decorating and less time passing around that damn bottle of Jameson, we'd have a more even distribution."

Another year had passed, and as always, the Collins cousins had just finished consuming their obnoxiously huge Friendsgiving dinner. They were now gathered in the living room of the apartment above Pat's Pub, decorating the Christmas tree.

This year, there'd been a slight break in tradition as they were celebrating Friendsgiving the Saturday *after* Thanksgiving, rather than the one before, thanks to a nasty flu bug in Yvonne and Darcy's household last week, taking down their husbands, Leo and Ryder, as well as Yvonne's baby daughter, Reba. Both women had been distraught over missing the event, so they'd all agreed to postpone it a week.

Friendsgiving was probably one of Oliver's top five favorite days of the year. While he enjoyed doing Thanksgiving with his entire family, there was something about spending time with his cousins and close friends—all twenty- and thirty-somethings—that appealed to him just a little bit more. Probably because they were freer with the booze, the cussing, the drinking games—he'd just ruled at flip cup—as well as the risqué jokes and stories. Plus, with fewer family members in the room, he got to talk to everyone more. Not a day went by when Oliver wasn't grateful to be a part of this crazy, fun family.

"Hey, normally you're the one hogging the whiskey. It's not my fault you went and got knocked up," Oliver teased. Sunnie had shocked them all at Thanksgiving dinner when she said she was thankful for generous maternity leave. The next great-grandchild was coming in May, and Oliver couldn't be more thrilled for Sunnie and her husband, Landon.

Landon took another chug of Jameson and grinned when Sunnie narrowed her eyes at him. Landon was already three sheets to the wind, something that was pretty unusual for the straight-laced cop.

"What?" Landon said, giving his wife an innocent look that missed the mark by a mile. "I'm drinking for two now."

Sunnie laughed loudly and grabbed another ornament, muttering, "asshole," before returning to the tree.

Oliver gave up on taking ornaments from the pile and instead started shifting some of the lower ones higher. He turned and caught sight of Gavin kicked back in the recliner, enjoying the show. "Thanks for the help, bro," he said sarcastically.

Gavin raised one eyebrow. "You all look like a bunch of ants scurrying around a sugar cube. I'm not even attempting to break into that mess."

Erin, Oliver's girlfriend, came out of the kitchen with a tray full of mugs of homemade eggnog. Oliver quickly walked over to grab one before the vultures descended and there was none left.

Erin made killer eggnog, using, as she said, "fresh-from-the-chicken's-butt eggs" from Leo's family's farm.

Oliver and Erin had been dating just over a year, his first truly serious girlfriend, and the more time that passed, the more convinced he was that she was the one.

Unfortunately, she wasn't the *only* one he wanted.

Gavin, who wouldn't budge for the tree decorating, stood quickly to help himself to one of the mugs of eggnog before relieving her of the heavy tray.

"Thanks," Erin said, before pointing at Gavin's glass. "By the way, that's your third one."

"You're keeping count?" Gavin asked. "You can't keep your eyes off me, can you?"

Erin rolled her eyes at his joke. "Don't you wish."

"Actually, I'm afraid you're lacking..." Gavin said, slowly shaking his head as he gestured toward his crotch with his mug hand, while trying to hold steady the eggnog tray with the other.

"Oh, that's right. I don't have a penis," Erin said. And then, because she and Gavin were professionals when it came to teasing each other, she added, "Phew. Dodged that bullet."

Gavin chuckled and gave her the win, placing the tray on the coffee table before resuming his seat in the recliner.

"Sunnie," Erin said, lifting up one of the mugs. "I made an alcohol-free one for you."

Sunnie's eyes lit up. "Yes! Although I'm going to pretend it has rum in it. Between Landon and my dad, I don't know how I'm going to make it six more months without alcohol. I swear they've found a way to double-down on their overprotectiveness. Something I seriously didn't think was possible. To make matters worse, Dad actually called me this morning and spent twenty minutes lecturing me on the importance of prenatal vitamins. I had to put my foot down when he started to launch into the pros and cons of natural childbirth, reminding him he was a cop and not a doctor."

Erin laughed. "I think it's great your dad is so excited."

"That's because you're watching it from afar," Layla said. "You just wait until *we* start having babies. The Morettis are going to be just as insanely annoying."

Layla, Erin's cousin, was dating Oliver's cousin, Finn. Gavin constantly joked that the blending of the two families was unavoidable, considering half the East Coast seemed to be related to either the Collinses of Baltimore or the Morettis of Philadelphia. As such, Gavin had determined their dating pools were seriously limited, and overlapping was bound to occur.

"I didn't say they wouldn't be annoying," Erin said, "but the fact that they live in Philly might help mitigate some of that."

Miguel—Layla and Finn's third—snorted, then pretend-sneezed the word, "Bullshit."

Finn slapped his boyfriend on the shoulder. "Amen to that. The Moretti brothers might live in another state, but they still find ways to make their presence known."

Layla rolled her eyes. "My brothers are fine...now."

"*Now* being the operative word," Miguel added.

Layla was the youngest and only girl in a family of five, and her older brothers had taken some time warming up to the fact their kid sister was shacking up with not one but two men. However, it had been two years now, and the Moretti brothers had not only accepted the relationship, but they'd welcomed Finn and Miguel into their fold...and joined the Collins clan at the same time.

Erin handed out the rest of the eggnog, Colm and Kelli each grabbing a glass. Most of the cousins—the ones with kids—had headed home after dessert, but more than a few of them had opted to hang out longer to help decorate the Christmas tree.

Oliver missed the days when there were a lot of cousins living in the apartment that Aunt Riley had dubbed the Collins Dorm. As the youngest of the cousins, Oliver had waited impatiently for years to be old enough to finally move in. Of course, by the time he'd gotten there, most of the others had fallen in love and moved out. Right now, it was only he and Gavin sharing the too-big space that had once been the home Pop Pop shared with Grandma Sunday and their seven kids. Oliver swore that one day it was going to be *his* family, his own hopefully huge brood, filling this apartment.

As he glanced at Gavin and Erin, he felt—as he always did—that spark of hope that it would be the two of them living here with him. And while there was no indication that would ever work out, Oliver was nothing if not an optimist. He got that personality trait from his father, Sean, who'd gotten it from Pop Pop.

Erin perched on the arm of Gavin's recliner, the two of them sipping eggnog and watching the family continue to jostle for a position around the tree as they added ornament after ornament —each of them containing some memory or story of years gone by—until they reached the final four.

Padraig carefully held up the box that contained the special ornaments, and he took off the lid.

"Hang on," Sunnie said, grabbing her phone. "I promised Pop Pop we'd FaceTime him when we got to this part."

Their elderly grandfather now lived with Sunnie's parents, Riley and Aaron. They'd added an "in-law" style suite to their house when Pop Pop's knees got too bad to continually make the trek up and down the stairs that led from the pub to this apartment.

"Hey, Pop Pop. What do you think?" Sunnie asked as she held the phone up to show him the tree as Colm plugged in the lights.

"Oh my. What a bonny tree. I think that might be the best one we've ever had," Pop Pop said.

Oliver and Gavin shared a grin. Pop Pop said the exact same thing every year.

"We've got Grandma Sunday's ornaments here." Sunnie

turned her phone to show him the box, which Padraig had placed on the coffee table.

Pop Pop referred to them as the "family's treasure," as if they were a band of pirates and this was their buried booty. Oliver doubted there was anyone in the family who couldn't recite the story of how Pop Pop and Sunday had been so poor during their first Christmas in America that they hadn't even been able to afford ornaments for their Charlie Brown-style tree.

According to Pop Pop, Sunday had found a box of lightbulbs, which she'd painted with bright, festive, colorful holiday scenes. Somehow, every single one of those glass ornaments had survived countless decades—which was no small miracle, considering how rowdy the Collins boys could get—and they were always the last ornaments to be placed on the tree.

Sunnie held the phone as Colm, Finn, Padraig, and Oliver each took one from the box.

When Oliver's dad lived here with his siblings, the honor of hanging the ornaments belonged to Sunday, and then, after her passing, Pop Pop. However, since then, the cousins had begun to take turns because Pop Pop refused to take the ornaments with him when he moved out, insisting that they belonged in Sunday's home.

This year was Oliver's turn, but as his gaze landed on Gavin, who gave him a thumbs-up and a wink that didn't hide the fact he was as touched as the others in this room by the annual tradi-tion, he decided to add someone new to the rotation.

Oliver held out the ornament he held. "Your turn this year, Gavin."

Gavin appeared surprised as he looked at Colm, Padraig, and Finn.

"Get up here, cuz," Padraig said, gesturing for Gavin to join them.

Gavin stepped next to Oliver, not bothering to hide his surprise...and gratitude. "You sure?"

Oliver handed him the ornament. "Don't drop it," he joked, though the huskiness of his voice lessened the effect.

"Thanks," he said, low enough Oliver was certain he was the only one to hear it.

Oliver wondered how long it would take for Gavin to believe he truly was a part of this family. He'd lived amongst them for nine years now, but even after all that time, the memories of his mother and the trauma caused by her physical and mental abuse still cast a wide shadow over his life.

Oliver lightly hip-bumped him and smiled. "You belong here, brother."

"Okay, you guys ready?" Sunnie held the phone up so Pop Pop could watch as each of them placed the ornaments on the tree. They'd purposely kept a section front and center clear of ornaments so that these would stand out. One by one, they added them to the tree, and as they did so, Sunnie led them in a round of "We Wish You a Merry Christmas." Oliver could hear Pop Pop's voice bellowing out the words through the phone.

Once all the ornaments were in place, they stood back to admire their work.

"Best tree yet," he heard Pop Pop say before bidding them all good night.

After that, the rest of the family began to leave until it was just Gavin, Oliver, and Erin left in the apartment. She topped up each of their mugs with the last of the eggnog, and the three of them sat together watching the tree lights flicker.

Oliver and Erin cuddled on the couch as Gavin reclaimed his spot in the recliner. Oliver wondered how many nights in the past year the three of them had been right here, just like this. He'd started dating Erin shortly before Friendsgiving last year, their relationship becoming more serious shortly after the holidays.

"I thought Zach was coming to Friendsgiving tonight," Erin said, glancing at Gavin.

Gavin never seemed at a loss to find guys to date, but none of them lasted long.

"No. That's over. Guy was too over-the-top dramatic. Sort of wore me out."

Erin laughed softly even as she rolled her eyes. "You're too picky."

"Naw. All the good gay guys have already been snatched up."

Oliver felt Gavin's eyes on him as he spoke. Erin didn't miss the look either.

"You could always come to the dark side and find yourself a girlfriend like me," Oliver joked.

"Do it. Do it," Erin chanted, deepening her voice, as if she were some Disney villain luring the hero to evil.

Gavin waved them off. "Gay. Not bi. Remember?"

Oliver sighed and looked away for a moment, wishing he could find some way to move beyond these damn dreams. He had Erin now. That should be enough.

No. It *was* enough. It was.

Maybe if he told himself that enough times, he'd start to believe it.

Erin, bless her, always found a way to distract him from his heavy thoughts. "Oh, I forgot to tell you. Jordan moved out this morning."

"I thought she was staying in the apartment until the New Year?" Gavin mused.

Erin shrugged. "Decided she wanted to spend the holidays with her new beau at their place."

"Are we taking bets on how long it takes until the relationship fails and she comes back?" Oliver asked, completely ready to put money down on it. The gambling gene ran deep in the Collins family.

Erin shook her head. "Hell no. I'm not doing that again. I'm putting out feelers for a new roommate on Monday. Jordan needs to learn she can't keep screwing me like this. She falls in love in a hot minute, moves in with the loser, falls out of love in the next minute, then comes back to me with her tail between her legs, begging for her old room. Do you know how many months' rent she's screwed me out of with this game? I can't afford her anymore."

Oliver nodded, feigning support, even as he knew Erin's words were merely bravado. There wasn't a doubt in his mind she'd take Jordan back because Erin had a heart as big as New York and softer than a marshmallow.

"You know, you could always give up your place and move in here with us."

If he'd been a smart man, he would have broached that subject with Gavin first, and privately, but he'd had one too many mugs of eggnog, and his mouth was working faster than his brain. Still, neither he nor Erin missed the sudden change in expression on Gavin's face.

He had to hand it to his foster brother. He schooled it quickly, but for a split second, there was no missing the frown... or was it a scowl?

Shit.

Luckily, Erin knew how to save him from himself. "Hell no. Y'all are slobs, and while I don't mind visiting this testosterone-laden abode from time to time, it's nice to have a chance to escape it at the end of the day."

"Speaking of escapes," Gavin added. "I'm done in. Think I'll call it a night. See you in the morning." He rose from the recliner, carrying his empty mug to the kitchen.

Neither Oliver nor Erin spoke until they heard him walk down the hall, closing his bedroom door behind him.

"Oops," Oliver mumbled.

Erin shook her head, but her gentle smile told him she wasn't mad at him. It was one of the things he loved the most about her. She was slow to anger, quick to forgive, and the most patient person he'd ever known. He'd dated enough high-maintenance women to appreciate Erin's easygoing approach to life. "I know you say you've moved on, Ollie—"

"I *have* moved on."

Erin shook her head, refusing to accept what they both knew was a lie. "I know what you want, but Gavin doesn't want the same."

"I don't—" he started.

She cut him off with a wave of her hand. "You've said I'm enough, Ollie. And I believe you. But I also know there's still a part of you that longs for more. You don't have to hide that from me."

Oliver ran his hand through his hair, frustrated. "Erin," he started.

"Don't," Erin cut in. "Don't pretend for me. We've been together long enough that I know you still harbor that dream of a relationship like the one your parents share. And I also know you keep trying to put me and Gavin in those roles."

Oliver shook his head, refusing to admit that because he didn't want to hurt her, didn't want her to think that what they shared wasn't enough for him. He'd already lost Gavin to this dream. He couldn't lose her too.

Part of him wondered if his inability to accept his dreams couldn't come to fruition was hindered by Erin and Gavin's friendship. It was so genuine, so close. When he'd first started dating Erin, it hadn't taken long to know she was special, different from the women he'd dated before.

Gavin had realized—even before Oliver—that Erin was going to stick. The first couple of months had been touch and go as Gavin's mood whenever Erin was around plummeted, his foster brother acting like a grade-A moody, sullen asshole. It had gotten so bad that Oliver had even briefly considered breaking things off with her, hating the feeling of having to choose between his girlfriend and his best friend.

In the end, it had been Erin who'd turned the tide. She'd looked right at Gavin shortly before Valentine's Day last year and asked him point-blank why he didn't like her.

Gavin hadn't had an answer, at least not one he was willing to confess. He'd closed down in true Gavin style, reverting to character, and Oliver had stepped in to whisk Erin away before she pushed him too far.

However, Erin stood her ground and asked Gavin to give her a chance—a real chance—and to Oliver's surprise, his friend had apologized for acting like a jerk and agreed.

After that...things got a lot easier.

At least for Erin and Gavin.

They'd become such great friends that there were times when Oliver felt like the damn outsider. Not that he was complaining.

Much.

"Sometimes I wonder..." Erin said, pausing. She bit her lower lip, and Oliver got a sense she regretted what she'd just started to say. "Never mind."

"You wonder what?" he pressed.

"I wonder if you and I had never met...if you and Gavin would have..."

Oliver sighed. There were no secrets between him and Erin. He'd fallen for her just as quickly as her roommate Jordan fell for her flavors of the month. Layla had introduced him to her cousin shortly after Erin had landed a nursing job at Johns Hopkins in the E.R., making the move from Philly to Baltimore. Oliver had taken one look at the curvy brunette with chocolate-brown eyes and known he'd met his soulmate.

Well...one of them.

Erin's hot-blooded Italian mother had met and fallen madly in love with her hard-working and hard-playing Irish husband, and the result had been Erin Cafferty. Like him, she laughed loudly and often, spoke her mind, rarely flashed her fiery temper —but when she did, watch out—and once they'd committed to this relationship, she'd been all in, holding back nothing.

As such, she knew all about Ollie's wild dreams, his desire to find a relationship just like that of his parents. Erin was as open-minded and adventurous as they came. Unlike the Moretti brothers, Erin had been quick to accept Layla's relationship with both Finn and Miguel, confiding to him early on that she'd thought it was "very cool and totally hot," and how she couldn't imagine anything better than finding true love with not just one person but two. She'd told him she would be open to that kind of relationship if it was what he truly wanted.

If Oliver hadn't already fallen for her before, that would have sealed the deal for him.

Erin had also heard all of Oliver's "past lovers" stories, just as he'd heard hers, so she knew about his one night with Gavin and how it had ended. Why it had ended. Oliver had tried to convince her that he'd since come to realize that dream of a threesome relationship was just that...a dream.

But every now and then, like tonight, he'd slip up and reveal more than he should, and once more, she'd be left to wonder if she truly was enough. He hated doing that to her.

He'd let his dreams keep him and Gavin apart, so how could he expect her to believe the same wouldn't hold true in their relationship? While he'd sworn to her that wouldn't happen, it was clear she didn't believe him.

"You know Gavin and I..." He started to say hooked up, but that felt too impersonal, especially given his feelings for Gavin.

"Slept together," Erin finished when he stumbled. "I know that, but—"

"But nothing. It was just one time and we both knew afterwards that...it wasn't enough. That something was missing."

The truth was his night with Gavin had been fucking amazing. The only other lover he'd ever taken to bed who'd rocked his world like that was Erin. But Oliver had fucked it up when he'd misread the entire thing with Gavin, planning a future out loud for the two of them and some unknown woman.

"Nothing was missing in Gavin's mind," Erin softly reminded him.

He knew that. But it didn't change the facts. "It wouldn't work, Erin. I want a wife and babies."

"And a husband. Gavin."

Oliver hadn't planned to add anything else to that list because he'd made that mistake once before. Lost someone he loved because his dreams were too big, too wild. But Erin wouldn't let him lie. Not even to himself. Because she was right.

He didn't just want a wife.

He wanted it all.

❈ 3 ❈

"Thanks for letting me know, Aaron." Gavin stood at the doorway of the pub and watched Aaron Young cross the street and climb back into his police cruiser. He'd only just gotten home from work when he'd been waylaid by his foster uncle, a cop with the Baltimore police department, on the sidewalk outside.

He'd intended to head straight upstairs to the dorm, shower, and hit the couch, but given the information he'd just gotten, he thought a beer—maybe several—sounded a lot better.

Gavin walked to the bar, claiming a stool, suddenly feeling very tired. He'd actually come home from work in a good mood, feeling almost chipper as he recalled Friendsgiving and how he'd been invited to put one of Grandma Sunday's ornaments on the tree. For a kid who'd grown up with fuck all in terms of family traditions—unless he counted his mother's dark days and the beatings—being included in that one had made him feel like a man who'd won a billion-dollar lottery.

Padraig came over and pointed to the Guinness tap.

Gavin nodded. He'd lived in the apartment upstairs for a few years now, which meant Padraig had gotten damn good at knowing what drink he needed when. Padraig slid the full pint glass in front of him.

Gavin sighed, lifted it, and took a long swig. Then he noticed Emmy looking up from her computer. He caught her eye and nodded by way of hello. "Missed you the other night at Friends-giving, Emmy," he said.

She smiled and pointed to her computer. "Facing the deadline from hell. Wrote until the wee hours that night. Still not done."

"Told her I'm going to put her on a daily word count regime so she doesn't get this behind again." Padraig pretended to crack a whip. "Write, wench, write!" he joked.

Emmy rolled her eyes and pointed to her empty glass. "Wine, barkeep, wine!"

He topped her glass up, then returned to Gavin when Emmy looked back at her computer screen, her fingers flying over the keys once more. Gavin couldn't begin to understand how Emmy, a romance writer, was able to concentrate in the loud bar, but she swore the place had become her muse, feeding her stories.

"Was that Aaron I saw you talking to outside?" Padraig asked.

"Yeah. He, uh, had some news for me."

Padraig studied his face but didn't ask what news. He was giving Gavin the chance to decide if he wanted to share or not. Padraig's quiet nature was what made him a very good bartender...and friend. Ever since turning twenty-one, Gavin had found himself sitting at this bar many a night, just because he enjoyed talking to Padraig.

Gavin had very few confidantes because he found it difficult to share things about himself and his past. Oliver had been the first person he'd opened up to, and then slowly, over time, he'd felt safe revealing more of himself to Sean, Lauren, and Chad.

Lately, he'd been thinking he would like to talk to Erin about his childhood. Erin was the first "girl" friend he'd ever had, as he'd always preferred the company of guys. Sometimes he wondered if that was because his experience with females was pretty much limited to his mother, and God knew he didn't talk to her about... anything. Not unless he wanted it used against him.

The main problem with confiding in Erin was that when the subject of him and Oliver being foster brothers had initially come up, he'd made some comment about his mother being gone for good—which Erin had misinterpreted as she was dead—and he hadn't corrected her because it was still hard for him to talk about...fuck...*anything* personal.

Gavin had decided to let Erin continue to believe what she did because with his mother locked away, he could pretend he'd always been a part of the Collins family and had something resembling a normal life.

What a joke.

Gavin had stopped trying to get his mom out of the hospital near the end of his first year with the Collins family. Prior to that, he'd been determined to "save her," convinced that it was his job to take care of her, that she couldn't make it on her own without him. Primarily because his mother had always told him she couldn't. And he'd believed her.

While logically, he knew he'd only been a kid when he suffered the worst of his mother's abuse, it was still hard for him —as a man—to admit to ever being so weak, so helpless, so manipulated.

The problem was, his mom hadn't always been horrible. When she was lucid, she tried. Tried to hold down a job, to pay the bills, to be a good mother. Or, well...maybe it was better to say she just tried to be a mother.

Yeah. The fact she was out was bad. *Really* bad.

His feelings for his mother were—and always had been—a jumble, something he'd never managed to sort out in any way that made sense to him. If she'd just been a mean drunk, it would have been easier to explain away her abuse, but it wasn't the alcohol—or just the alcohol—that drove her actions. And then there were those days when she'd been nice to him.

He'd known this day was coming. Maybe he hadn't wanted to admit it to himself, but he'd known. She'd always been there, in the back of his mind.

Unbeknownst to everyone—Oliver included—when he'd gotten his driver's license, Gavin had begun making two trips to the psychiatric hospital a year, once on his mother's birthday and again on Christmas Eve. He would drop off a package, usually containing nothing more than some snacks, magazines, books, stuff like that for her. He never included a card and he never gave it to her personally, unwilling to face her.

"You okay, Gavin?" Padraig asked when the silence lasted too long.

Over the years, Padraig had been slowly indoctrinated into Gavin's small group of confidantes. And Gavin now realized he'd eschewed the trip upstairs because he wanted to talk to Padraig as much as he wanted the beer.

"It was about my mother."

"Okay." Padraig frowned, looking concerned. His compassion —something the entire Collins family seemed to have in spades —went a long way toward soothing the burn of the scab Aaron had just ripped off. "What about her?"

From Padraig's dark tone, it was apparent the bartender was ready to step in as the first line of defense if Gavin asked.

"She's out." It was just two words, but damn if they didn't cut through Gavin sharper than any knife could.

"Fuck," Padraig muttered.

"Yeah."

Gavin took another sip of beer and stretched his neck muscles, trying to loosen the knots in his shoulders that tightened the second Aaron had told him his mother had been released from the state mental hospital that morning.

Jesus.

Five minutes after getting the news and he was wound up tighter than a spring.

While Aaron didn't know as much about Gavin's childhood as Oliver and Padraig, he'd known the reason why Gavin had been placed with Sean, Lauren, and Chad. Cops tended to know all the details when one of their own was hurt.

"You think she'll try to contact you?"

Gavin shrugged. "I have no idea what she'll do. I haven't seen or spoken to my mother since I was fifteen."

Not that he hadn't tried to contact her during his first year with the Collins family. He'd escaped his bedroom countless times, sometimes hitching rides, sometimes stealing money from his foster family to pay cab fare to the hospital. He was turned away every single time, and then Sean, Lauren, or Chad—after a call from the security guard—would come pick him up and bring him back home.

The last time he'd seen his mom, he had come home to find the shitty apartment he shared with her filled with cops and EMTs and, unsurprisingly, his social worker, Margie.

He'd run out of the house an hour or so earlier—*chased* out was probably more accurate—when he had come home from school to discover his mother in the midst of one of her rages.

She'd pulled a knife on him, something she had never done before. Even now, Gavin could recall the guilt he'd felt for month afterwards, blaming himself for her use of a weapon.

After all, he'd been the one who'd thought the fact he'd grown several inches taller and put on some serious muscle weight, thanks to his strength-training class at school, should serve as a deterrent to her beatings. So the last time she'd backhanded him, a few months prior to that night, he'd gotten cocky and told her that was the last time she threw a punch that he didn't return.

In her rage, she'd decided to prove to him she would always be top dog—hence the weapon. He'd walked in after school and she'd launched into one of her tirades, his attention drawn to the empty bottle of gin laying on the floor. She'd screamed at him, called him a piece of shit and a bastard and a whole host of other things he'd heard a million times before when she was deep in the grips of the alcohol or her depressed rages.

Then she'd picked up a knife he hadn't noticed, from the end table, and gotten one good slice in his shoulder before he managed to swing his bookbag at her, knocking the weapon out of her hands. While she'd lunged to grab it, he'd run out of the apartment, deciding to make himself scarce until she passed out. He'd only managed to stay away an hour or so because the wound on his arm wouldn't stop bleeding and he had needed proper bandages.

His world had been blown to bits when he'd arrived home to discover the shit had hit the fan. Margie pulled him aside to say one of the neighbors had called the police about their fight. Two cops came to check out the disturbance, and his mother had stabbed one of them in the arm several times before his partner could pull her off.

Gavin had been taken to the hospital where they'd put ten stitches in his arm, then he'd spent that night in a group home. The next morning, Margie had delivered him to Sean, Chad, and Lauren's house.

His mother had been committed to the state psychiatric hospital. In addition to her alcohol addiction and depression, his mother had been diagnosed with antisocial personality disorder, which had given her defense attorney a way to keep her out of prison.

"Given what you've said about her, I'm surprised they let her out," Padraig said.

Gavin wished *he* was. But he should have known his luck wouldn't last. "She's a sociopath and a drunk, but I guess they couldn't hold her forever. Even though it would be better for everyone if they would."

Not everyone...just him.

There must have been more malevolence in his tone than

he'd intended, because Emmy's gaze lifted from her laptop, her brows rose in surprise.

He never lost his temper, refusing to unleash his anger on others around him. He wouldn't be his mother.

"Sorry, Emmy," he murmured.

She smiled. "I'm sorry for eavesdropping. Bad habit."

Padraig snorted. "Never heard you admit to that before."

She narrowed her eyes at him. "I was talking to Gavin. Not you."

"Pot, meet kettle," Gavin teased, grateful to have the chance to change the subject.

Padraig and Emmy laughed and acknowledged they were both accomplished eavesdroppers.

Gavin sighed. He needed time to wrap his head around the fact his mom was out. Though Lauren had offered to take him to visit his mom after he turned eighteen, Gavin had refused, unwilling to face her again after so many years. He figured the biannual gifts were enough, a simple way of appeasing the guilt he felt over abandoning her.

For the last couple of years, all he'd felt in regards to his mom was the guilt tied to his hope that he'd never have to see her again, never have to face her anger over him leaving her alone for so long.

Nine years hadn't been long enough to sort out his emotions for the woman, and now...fuck. Now he was going to have to face the demons—well, *the* demon—of his past. Because he didn't doubt for a second, she was going to find him, whether he wanted to be found or not.

Emmy went back to typing and Padraig studied his face for a moment. "If you need to talk..." he offered.

Gavin smiled. "I appreciate that, but..."

"Not tonight?"

Gavin shook his head. "I gotta figure some shit out first."

"Alrighty then. New subject. Where's the rest of your gang?" Padraig asked.

Gavin wasn't sure he'd refer to him, Oliver, and Erin as a gang. More like a couple, plus one, but he rolled with it. "Date night."

"Oh, damn, that's right. It's Tuesday. Not sure where I lost a day this week. I keep thinking it's Monday. Hey, Em, remind me Seamus has a vet appointment tomorrow afternoon," Padraig called out.

"On it," she said without looking up.

Gavin had always admired Padraig and Emmy's close friendship. She'd begun hanging out at the pub a couple years earlier, claiming a spot at the end of the bar. Padraig had actually had a nameplate made for her, so that her seat was permanently reserved.

"I swear to God that dog gets more contrary by the day," Padraig said.

"He's spoiled," Gavin pointed out. It was common knowledge to basically everyone in the family that no dog had ever been more loved.

"Blame Mia for that. I'm pretty sure if I'd asked her, she would have said Seamus was her soul mate and the two of them were just doing me a favor, letting me live in their apartment. You know, I'm still finding unopened dog toys that she bought for him stuffed in random, weird places. It's like she was determined to make sure she remained Seamus's favorite forever. Because damn if that dog doesn't know when it's a present from Mia." Padraig chuckled as he shook his head.

Gavin laughed. "Mia was awesome, and she did love that dog."

Padraig nodded, still smiling, and it occurred to Gavin that lately whenever Mia's name came up, the sadness that used to pervade Padraig's face was no longer there. He was able to talk about his late wife with happiness, to remember her without drifting to a dark place.

Then Gavin realized Emmy wasn't typing anymore. Instead,

she was looking at Padraig. And the sadness that was missing from the bartender's face was written all over hers.

The Collins family placed bets on everything under the sun, but the one thing none of them seemed willing to wager on was when Emmy would come clean and tell Padraig how she felt. It felt too personal, too raw. Too...serious to be made light of.

"So, how's your love life?" Padraig asked, wiping the counter.

Gavin glanced around and realized the place was pretty empty at the moment. The majority of the business was next door on Sunday's Side as the happy hours had faded into dinnertime, so obviously Padraig was looking for some company himself.

"Nonexistent," Gavin said.

The lights flickered for a minute, and Padraig shook his head. "Damn." Then he counted, "Three, two, one."

Just as he hit one, Riley came into the pub. "Goddammit," she said as she approached the bar. "I did it again."

Padraig grinned as he stepped out from behind the counter and headed toward the storage closet in the back. "Yeah. I figured that out. Be right back."

"What's going on?" Gavin asked.

"One of the outlets in the kitchen stopped working. I keep overloading the ones that *do* work and flipping the breaker. Poor Paddy's had to run to the storage closet four times today to flip it back," Riley explained. "Ewan's got a call in to an electrician, but he can't get here until early next week."

Gavin tilted his head. "And it never occurred to you to ask *me* to take a look?"

Riley waved him away. "You just got home from work. It's fine."

"Riley—" Gavin started.

"All fixed," Padraig said, rejoining them.

"Thanks, Paddy." Then Riley put her hands on her hips when she saw his pint glass. "You have dinner yet?"

He shook his head. He'd intended to head straight up to the

apartment, but he'd been waylaid by the news about his mother and then annoyed enough that beer sounded better than food. "I'll microwave some soup when I get upstairs."

"Canned soup?"

He nodded.

"No, you won't. Stay there. Canned soup..." she muttered with disgust. "I'll bring you *real* soup."

"What about the outlet?" he asked.

"It'll keep until this weekend. You can fix it then," Riley called out over her shoulder.

Gavin grinned when Padraig reclaimed his position across the bar from him. "Apparently I'm having dinner down here tonight."

Padraig laughed. "You've been around enough years to know that food is love in Riley's world." He glanced up when the bell over the door jingled and a couple walked in. "Finally, some customers." Padraig grabbed a couple menus as he led the patrons to a table and took their drink order.

Riley returned with the food. "Eat," was all she said as she put the steaming bowl of cream of crab soup in front of him, along with a basket of fresh-baked rolls. His mouth watered just looking at it.

"Damn," he murmured appreciatively, which appeared to be all the thanks Riley needed. She patted him on the back and laughed before walking back to the kitchen.

Gavin made a mental note to get up early Saturday morning to fix her outlet for her. Doing construction, he'd had plenty of opportunities to work with the electricians they hired. He'd even considered doing a full-time apprenticeship to become a journeyman after high school, but Oliver was determined the two of them were going to take over the construction company together once Justin, Killian, and Sean retired. They needed to "keep it in the family," Oliver liked to say.

Gavin dug into the soup with gusto, savoring every single bite. Emmy continued to type away, her fingers racing over the keyboard the only sound besides the quiet chatter of the patrons scattered throughout the pub. As he ate, he realized he was no longer stressed out, and he knew exactly why.

No matter how long he remained with the Collins family, welcomed as one of their own, there was a part of him that simply never stopped being awed by their kindness. He'd spent too many of his formative years with a mother who fluctuated between abuser and taker.

His mother, who was fragile on good days, had been truly terrifying when in the midst of one of her black rages. It had taken years of being away from her before he realized that she'd never—not once—given him anything truly resembling what others considered motherly love. No hugs, smiles, or even a damn bowl of soup.

While his mom told him she loved him, it was always wrapped up in subtle controlling phrases like, "you're all I have" or "there's no one else to take care of me." And Gavin had soaked up those phrases, believing they were genuine professions of love, when in truth, they were simple manipulations to ensure Gavin cooked and cleaned—and even stole money when they were broke.

Too many times, he'd been moved out of the house when a teacher caught sight of his bruises. Some of the foster homes where he'd been placed prior to moving in with Sean, Lauren, and Chad hadn't been much better than the apartment he'd shared with his mom.

There were some people—like Oliver's parents—who were in the foster system for all the right reasons. Because they cared about kids, wanted to make a difference in someone's life, wanted to show children who'd been kicked to the curb that they were worthy of love. But there were just as many of the other kind. The ones who took in foster kids for the monthly check provided by CPS, and he'd lived with plenty of those during his childhood.

Gavin put some butter on one of the hot rolls and sighed

happily. He might not be used to the concept of mothering, but he sure as shit still loved the way Lauren and the Collins aunts continually offered him that kind of unconditional love.

He'd just finished dinner when he heard someone call his name.

"Hey, Gavin."

Glancing over his shoulder, he saw Layla waving to him to join her. Picking up his mug, he crossed the bar.

"Hey, Layla. What's up?"

"Just waiting on my fellas to get here. We decided to hell with dinner. We're ordering appetizers and drinks and calling it a night."

He laughed. "Rough day?"

Layla shrugged. "Not really. More like none of us felt like cooking and cleaning up. Did you already eat?"

"Had a bowl of Riley's cream of crab soup, but I wouldn't say no to some cheese fries if that's on your list of apps."

"Cheese fries are—and always will be—number one on the appetizer list. Sit down and join us." Layla looked up and smiled when Padraig placed a glass of wine in front of her. "The guys will be here in a minute. Miguel said he's in a PBR mood, which means Finn will want the same."

Padraig nodded, then pointed to Gavin's nearly empty glass. "Going in for a second round?"

"Hell yeah." Gavin thanked Padraig before he returned to the bar. "How are things at the coffee shop?"

Layla had moved away from Philadelphia and her large brood of brothers a couple years earlier after purchasing the Daily Grind, a coffee shop just a few blocks from the pub.

"The coffee business is always good...mercifully," she said.

"There you are." Miguel bent over and gave Layla a quick kiss on the cheek before claiming the chair on her right.

Finn was only a few steps behind him. "You're a sight for sore eyes," he murmured to Layla as he opted for a longer kiss on her lips.

"Good to see you, Gavin," Miguel said. "You joining us for app night?"

He nodded. "Layla promised me cheese fries."

Finn laughed. "That's my girl. I'm starving. Might need two plates of fries tonight."

Gavin leaned back, enjoying the easy conversation as they all talked about work, the upcoming holidays, and the sudden chill in the weather. Finn and Miguel helped Layla brainstorm gift ideas for her brothers.

Gavin watched the way the three of them were with each other, the relationship reminding him of the one shared by his foster parents. Before coming to live with Lauren, Sean, and Chad, Gavin had never considered, never even realized, people could live in committed threesome relationships, but there was no denying that it worked for all of them.

Oliver hoped for the same relationship. Hell, his best friend hoped for the same relationship with *him*—but Gavin wasn't wired that way. And he was convinced the reason Layla, Finn, and Miguel's relationship worked was because they were all *together*. They weren't two separate couples trying to blend into a threesome.

Gavin was gay, and yes, he was attracted to—and probably in love with—Oliver more than he cared to admit. And while Oliver had feelings for him too, he was just as much in love with Erin. The problem was, Gavin and Erin could never be anything more than friends. And try as he might, Gavin couldn't see that working in the long term.

What if jealously emerged somewhere down the road?

Or what if one of the couples fell out of love?

What would keep the three of them together?

They finished their appetizers and Finn paid the bill, refusing to allow Gavin to chip in, so he promised the next time was on him.

"Are we missing a party?"

Gavin looked up at the sound of Oliver's voice, surprised to discover he and Erin weren't alone.

"Look who we found outside," Erin said.

Gavin forced a smile when he spotted Brad, a male nurse who worked with Erin at Hopkins. Brad had discovered the pub a few months ago, and since then, he'd become somewhat of a regular.

"Hey, Brad," Gavin said.

"Not sure you missed a party, but I'm afraid you missed the cheese fries," Layla said with a yawn. "We were just heading home. I gotta be up early to open the shop."

She, Finn, and Miguel all rose and, after a few minutes of chatting with Erin and Oliver, they said their goodbyes.

"The three of us were going to grab some stools at the bar and have a drink," Oliver said. "Want to keep going?"

Gavin considered it, then shook his head, as Erin and Brad claimed their seats, the two of them laughing over something Padraig said that Gavin didn't hear.

Brad was a good-looking guy, with a good sense of humor. He was also bi. As Gavin watched him with Erin, it occurred to him that Brad would be the perfect third in Oliver and Erin's relationship.

Maybe he should give them some time alone to figure that out.

"No, man," he said at last. "I'm kind of tired. Think I'll call it a night."

Oliver looked ready to persist, but Gavin must have given him a look that proved it would be fruitless. "Okay. We're just having one. Erin and I will be up in a half an hour."

"Take your time. Brad's a good guy, a lot of fun."

Oliver rolled his eyes. "Stop."

Gavin narrowed his eyes. "What?"

"We don't need you playing matchmaker."

Gavin lifted one shoulder casually. "Don't know what you're talking about."

"Mmmhmm," Oliver hummed.

Gavin brushed Oliver's suspicions aside. "I'm grabbing a shower and then hitting the sheets."

"I'll see you in the morning then." Oliver walked to the bar, claiming the spot next to Brad. The other man placed his hand on the back of Oliver's high-backed stool and leaned in to say something. Oliver cracked up, his loud, boisterous, infectious laughter filling the pub.

Typically, the sound made Gavin laugh as well, but tonight it just made him...sad.

Then he thought about his mother, and his mood darkened even more.

Just like that, the tension was back in his shoulders.

"Fuck," he murmured.

Fuck it all.

$$\text{4}$$

Erin wiped the kitchen counter, while Gavin put the leftovers in the fridge. It was Friday, which meant dinner and a movie at home with Erin and Oliver, a tradition they'd started shortly after Valentine's Day, when Erin had asked Gavin to give her a chance. Nowadays, he struggled to remember a time when she wasn't one of his best friends, and he was ashamed of himself for acting like such a tool at the beginning.

They'd just polished off the better part of the beef stew Erin had made—God, she could cook—and Oliver had slipped away to grab a shower and change out of his work clothes. Erin kept a drawer of comfy clothes in Oliver's room, and the first thing she'd done after arriving at their apartment was strip off her scrubs and don a soft, long-sleeved T-shirt and yoga pants. Knowing her, he figured she was about five minutes away from stripping off her bra as well.

She'd done enough sleepovers with Oliver that Gavin was used to her unfastening her bra at random times and pulling the straps off through her shirt sleeves. He'd called it a cool trick the first couple of times she'd shed the lacy material without revealing so much as an inch of skin.

"You've been quiet tonight," she said, when Gavin pulled three beers from the refrigerator, popping the caps and handing her one. "You feeling okay?"

"Yeah. It's just been a long week." He was relieved his mother hadn't attempted to contact him. Then he figured she probably didn't know where he was or how to reach him.

If there was one thing that didn't exist in the Collins family, it was a secret. So Gavin appreciated that neither Padraig nor Aaron appeared to have told anyone else about his mom's release.

For the past few nights, he'd lain awake trying to imagine seeing her again, playing it out in his mind. He'd had years to consider their reunion, but as he'd grown older, the visions of it continually changed. When he was fifteen, all he'd wanted was to see her again, to go home. However, as more time passed, as he'd grown closer to Oliver, Sean, Lauren, and Chad, he'd started to see his childhood in a different light, and the anger, resentment, and guilt associated with those memories ate at him like cancer.

Right now, Gavin was torn between telling her off or... He swallowed heavily. He was terrified he'd revert to type and do what he'd always done.

Forgive her.

Give her a chance to make things up to him.

Reassume the caregiver role.

Gavin had never been able to hold on to his anger toward her, even after the most brutal of the beatings. Instead, she would shed what he now believed were crocodile tears, blame her anger on her loneliness or sadness, remind him he was all she had, and somehow, she'd always find a way to convince him the beating would never have happened if he hadn't done X, Y, or Z.

And in the end, because Gavin hated to see her cry, he'd tell her it was okay. Then, because he'd wanted the peaceful times to last, he'd go out of his way to take care of her, cooking meals, cleaning the apartment, stealing money and food.

Sometimes, he struggled to mesh the Gavin he'd been

growing up with the man the Collins family had raised him to be. None of them, not even Oliver, knew about the things he'd done to survive...or the things he might have done.

The night he'd run away from his mother after she'd sliced his arm with the knife, he'd been stopped by their creepy landlord and handed an eviction notice. The fucking asshole had insinuated he would look the other way on the late rent if Gavin blew him. Gavin had shoved the guy away, but he'd woken up in a cold sweat too many nights in the ensuing months, wondering if he would have gone through with it if the cops hadn't been called and his mom committed.

He couldn't believe how all of the shit going down around him had felt normal at the time.

Now, he was disgusted by it, even though deep inside, he knew he'd had no choice.

No. That was wrong.

He'd had a choice—he could have confided in his social worker or teachers, but he hadn't. Because in his young mind, there wasn't anything better on the other side.

Better the devil you knew and all that.

What was he going to say to his mom now? Too many times he'd played it out, imagined that this time, he would be able to unload every single hate-filled emotion on her, that he'd finally be able to tell her just how much she'd hurt him.

But he was terrified of unleashing all of that, of taking the lid off a fury he'd spent all of his life keeping bottled up.

He wouldn't be like his mother. He couldn't spew horrible things, couldn't inflict that much pain on someone he...

Fuck. Someone he loved.

How could he love her? How could he *still* love her after everything?

If he never saw her, he'd never have to risk losing sight of the man he'd become without her in his life.

So yeah...it would be a hell of a lot easier if the reunion never happened.

"You sure you're okay?" Erin asked, and he realized he'd let the silence between them linger a little too long.

He nodded, hoping she didn't see through the lie. Gavin hadn't told Oliver about his mother's release from the psychiatric hospital. It had been on the tip of his tongue to do so all week, but every time he opened his mouth to say it, he couldn't do it. Probably because his emotions were all over the fucking scale and he didn't know *what* to say.

As for Erin, well...he'd never said anything to her about his past or his mother other than she was gone forever, letting her assume his mom was dead.

Since the subject of his mother came up so infrequently, it really hadn't been an issue.

Until now.

"I'm sure. Just tired."

The two of them walked to the living room. Erin claimed her usual spot on the couch she shared with Oliver, while Gavin took the recliner. "Since you're not in a chatty mood, I think we should talk about me. Because as you know, everything about me is fascinating."

Gavin laughed, perfectly aware of why Oliver was so head over heels in love with her. Erin was genuinely fun to be with. She'd taken to calling him her best gay friend, while Oliver was her best boyfriend, and Layla, her best cousin friend. Erin liked to tease them, saying that she had so many best friends because she was, in her own words, "a goddamned national treasure."

And because she wasn't wrong, he, Oliver, and Layla always let the joke stand.

"Okay, so let's dive in here," he said. "What part of the Erin saga haven't we covered tonight, because I can't imagine there's much we've missed? You barely came up for air at dinner."

Erin had entertained him and Oliver at dinner with a recounting of her rather exciting workday in the E.R. Apparently three men had all been transported to the hospital, bloodied and bruised after an argument over a football game turned violent. The EMTs who'd responded to the call had erroneously believed the fight to be over, so when it erupted again in the waiting room, it had taken two doctors and three security guards to pull them all apart.

"The hunt for a roommate continues."

"No luck?"

She shook her head. "I've met with three women in the last week, and the fact that every single one of them sounded a different alarm makes me think I'm probably going to have to take Jordan back once she gets sick of her new boyfriend."

"What sort of alarms?"

"One woman asked about the hot water situation. Said she likes to take two forty-five-minute showers a day. What the hell could she do in a shower for an hour and half every day?"

Gavin wiggled his eyebrows. "I could probably come up with a list for you. How kinky do you want me to make it?"

"Gross. Pervert." She threw one of the throw pillows from the couch at him. He caught it midair and placed it behind his head.

"Another one wanted to know what size clothes and shoes I wore because she just loves sharing clothes with girlfriends. Given the fact she showed up in mom jeans and an ancient, stained hoodie, I'm pretty sure that sharing means she plans to invade my wardrobe because hers is crap. And the last one asked if I would be annoyed if she practiced her clarinet every night. Not to be rude, but who still plays the clarinet after ninth grade band class?"

Gavin chuckled. "Maybe you could take up the flute and the two of you could march around the pub. Give us a parade. Everyone loves parades," he said sarcastically.

"Everyone does *not* love parades," she retorted.

"Parade?" Oliver asked, clearly missing every part of their conversation, except the last word. "Are you talking about the Christmas one? Because if so, I'm in. I love parades." He picked up the beer Gavin had carried in for him as he sank down next to her, confused when she and Gavin cracked up laughing.

"I stand corrected," Gavin said, once he managed to pull himself together. "Ollie loves parades."

Oliver rolled his eyes, figuring out he was the butt of some joke, but he didn't care enough to find out what it was. Instead, he reached for the remote and fired up the movie.

They'd decided to watch Christmas movies every Friday night in December, and tonight's selection had been Gavin's choice, *Die Hard*, which he proclaimed was the greatest Christmas movie ever made. In honor of the viewing, he'd changed into the *Nakatomi Plaza 1988 Christmas Party* T-shirt Erin and Oliver had bought him last year for Christmas.

"Everybody ready?" Oliver asked.

Erin and Gavin nodded, and Oliver turned the lights off as they settled in to watch.

AFTER THE FIRST MOVIE, THE GUYS HAD BEEN SO PUMPED UP— there really was *so* much testosterone in this apartment—they'd opted to go ahead and watch the second. It was after midnight, and Gavin and Oliver were actually debating starting the third when Erin stood up. "I'm out. I was struggling to keep my eyes open during that last one."

Gavin shook his head. "You just don't appreciate good movies."

"Remember you said that when we watch my choice next week. Because contrary to what you think, *Love Actually* is *actually* the greatest holiday movie of them all."

Gavin groaned, but she knew he was full of bluster. She'd made them watch the movie with her last year and both men admitted—albeit reluctantly—that they had liked it.

"Yeah," Oliver said, yawning as he rose as well. "I'm tired too. Maybe we can keep the *Die Hard* marathon going tomorrow."

"Sounds like a great plan," she said. "I'm working the afternoon shift."

Gavin snorted but turned the TV off, the three of them drifting down the hall that led to Gavin and Oliver's bedrooms.

"Good night," Gavin called out when they walked into Oliver's room, and he continued on to his room at the end of the hall.

Oliver closed the door behind them, leaning against it, suddenly looking a lot less tired than he had in the living room.

"I thought you were tired," she teased. They'd been together long enough that she could read all his moods. She knew what sleepy looked like, and she knew what horny looked like.

Oliver was currently horny.

"Take off your clothes," he said, his voice suddenly husky. Just the sound of it had all thoughts of sleep vanishing from her mind.

And she *had* been sleepy.

Before Oliver, Erin had slept with four men, and she would have said she'd enjoyed sex with all of them. She'd been a fool.

Oliver took alpha to the next level in the bedroom, something she would never have suspected, given his laid-back attitude everywhere else. He'd introduced her to new positions, countless toys, bondage, sexy spankings, and a whole lot of other things that basically meant she was a raving nymphomaniac nowadays.

She reached for the bottom of her T-shirt and pulled it off. She had performed her bra-removal magic trick for the guys earlier, so with that one quick tug, she was completely topless. Oliver's eyes drifted to her breasts, and she could feel her nipples tightening in anticipation.

"I love your tits," he murmured, something he said to her pretty much every night.

She reached beneath them, cupping and lifting, giving him a little show as she slowly pinched her own nipples. Oliver was a big fan of her stripteases, so she always took care to make sure he got a good show.

Her eyes drifted closed as she pinched just hard enough to cross over the line from pleasure to pain.

"Eyes open," Oliver demanded.

Her eyelids lifted, and her gaze met his.

"Take off your pants and panties, sweet girl."

She loved when Oliver called her his sweet girl. She'd never really been a big fan of terms of endearment in dating—names like baby and honey and sweetheart always felt a bit sexist to her. And honestly, sweet girl definitely should have fallen into that same category, but with Oliver, it simply added to the sexual power exchange between them in the bedroom. She would never have pegged herself as a submissive lover before Oliver, but everything they did together turned her on in ways she couldn't have imagined.

She slid her pants and panties off together, toeing off her fuzzy socks as well. She stood in front of him, letting him look his fill. There was no embarrassment between them, no shyness. There never had been.

Erin was curvy—okay, chubby—but Oliver had never made her feel self-conscious about that. Instead, he looked at her like she was the most beautiful woman on the planet.

"You get more gorgeous every single day," he said, stepping closer.

She lifted herself up on tiptoe, tilting her head back for his kiss. Oliver had a good six inches on her height-wise. That, combined with his broad, muscular shoulders—his job working construction had honed his body until it was chiseled, rock hard, perfect—never failed to make her feel tiny, almost petite.

Oliver's kiss was rough, hungry. Sometimes, he liked to draw the foreplay out, keeping her on the edge of her orgasm for hours, until she was panting, begging. Other times, like tonight, his own needs were too strong and he gave into them, taking her hard, quick.

"Go lay down on the bed. Legs open."

She climbed into the middle of his mattress, giving him a bird's-eye view of exactly what she was offering. He shed his own clothing quickly before crawling over her body. He ran his fingers along her slit, grinning as he lifted his fingers and let her see how slick they were.

"Always so ready for me, sweet girl."

Erin wrapped her hands around his neck, trying to draw him down to resume their kisses, but he locked his arms, refusing to budge.

"Take my cock in your hand, Erin. Show me where you want me."

She reached between them, guiding him to her pussy.

"Please," she whispered.

He shifted until the head was lodged just inside her. "Need you so much tonight."

"Take me."

Oliver thrust deep, filling her in an instant. He didn't give her time to acclimate, to adjust. Instead, he gave her exactly what she wanted. He pounded inside her roughly, grasping her legs to lift her hips from the mattress, to open her even more for his passionate assault.

"God!" she cried when he stroked her clit with his thumb. Oliver knew exactly where and how to touch her, knew how to send her orbiting into space within minutes.

Her back arched and she saw stars as her orgasm exploded. Her climax didn't slow him down. He didn't miss a step, never paused for a moment, as he fucked her straight through it.

Erin used to insist she needed time to recover between, but Oliver had taught her differently, had shown her just how high he could push her. One orgasm morphed into a second, harder one.

She closed her eyes, cursing. "Fuck," she said through gritted teeth. "Fuck me."

Her nails scored his shoulders and she heard his hiss of pain. A drop of sweat rolled down his cheek and she reached up to wipe it away. He'd shaved during his shower, his face smoother, though it never really lost that rough sandpaper feel she adored.

Oliver's brown eyes held her gaze, and she was blown away by the unadulterated love she found there.

Oliver was her person. Her forever person.

If only...

Gavin's face flashed in her mind...just as it always did at this moment.

No matter how many times, how many ways she and Oliver came together like this, she always thought of *him* as they approached the end.

And she wasn't alone.

"I know," Oliver whispered. "He should be here with us. Say his name, sweet girl. Say it."

It was becoming their ritual lately. The first few times Oliver had made this demand, she'd refused. Not because she didn't want the same thing he did, but because she didn't believe it would happen.

God, she still didn't believe it.

It was easier for Oliver because Gavin *did* want him, *did* love him. She'd seen the glances the two men had exchanged, felt the longing between them.

Gavin didn't look at her that way. He never had. And he never would.

Regardless, Oliver had worn down the part of her that knew better than to bet on a long shot, that was careful with her heart. And so she gave him what he asked for.

"Gavin should be here," she whispered.

Oliver kissed her. "I love you, Erin," he said as his body tightened, a sign that he was close. Very close.

He stroked her clit again, determined to ring a third orgasm from her too-sensitive body.

"Ollie. God. Ollie!"

They came together as he dropped lower, kissing her through it.

"Yippee ki yay," he murmured, mimicking Bruce Willis from the movie, before withdrawing and shifting to her side. "I am never going to want to stop doing that. Gonna want to do that on my death bed."

She laughed. "You're insane. But yeah. Same. Can I go to sleep *now*?"

He kissed her on the cheek, turned off the lamp by the bed, and was probably asleep before she'd even managed to pull up the covers.

It felt like she'd just closed her eyes when the quiet, peaceful night was pierced by a painfully loud sound.

Oliver's eyes flew open, his hands reaching over to the nightstand to slap his cell phone. It took a second or two more before he realized it wasn't his phone that was blaring.

It was a fire alarm.

Erin was sitting up, looking around the room, as disoriented as him.

"What..." she said groggily.

He heard footsteps pounding down the hallway, and Gavin threw his bedroom door open so hard, it slammed against the wall, bounced off, and nearly closed on him again.

"Wake up!" Gavin said. "Fire."

Oliver jumped out of bed, searching for his pajama pants. He and Erin had fallen asleep after sex, both of them curling into each other's arms naked. As he pulled up his pants, he saw Gavin racing to the side of the bed, grabbing Erin's clothing off the floor as he did so. His foster brother was in the lounge pants and T-shirt he always slept in, barefoot.

Gavin pulled Erin's T-shirt over her shoulders as she slid to the edge of the bed.

"You gotta get up, Erin." Gavin gripped her upper arm firmly, helping her stand, then kneeled to help her into her yoga pants. Erin held on to his shoulders for support.

"Shoes..." Erin said, looking around the room.

"No time. Too much smoke already."

"Smoke?" Oliver had convinced himself it was a false alarm. He turned toward the hall and realized Gavin was right. The place was filling up with smoke...fast.

The three of them raced down the hall to the living room, the smoke even thicker in the large room. Oliver couldn't see flames, but his eyes were starting to water, to sting. "The fire must be down in the pub."

Fuck.

The fire was in the pub.

Oliver stood in the middle of the room as the reality of that crashed down on him hard.

"No time for this!" Gavin said, pushing Erin forward as he reached for Oliver's arm.

Gavin led them all to the fire escape and threw open the window. Glancing down into the alley behind the building, he turned and nodded. "It's safe. Come on. We'll have to go out this way. Won't make it through the pub if the fire is down there."

Erin stepped out onto the fire escape as Oliver heard the sound of sirens in the distance. Finn had installed a state-of-the-art alarm system a couple of years earlier after a rash of robberies in the neighborhood. The system not only detected break-ins but fire as well, which meant in addition to sending a message to the fire department, it would have blown up the phones of most of his aunts and uncles, and Padraig as well.

The system was also supposed to activate the sprinklers. He hoped they'd come on, and that was what accounted for all the smoke, sending up a prayer that perhaps the fire had already been contained or, even better, put out. However, given the incredible, unbearable heat coming up from the floor beneath him, he didn't hold on to that hope for long.

The moon shifted, peeking out from behind some clouds just

as Oliver reached the window. He glanced over his shoulder—and his stomach sank.

"Ollie. Come on!" Gavin shouted to be heard over the alarm. He had one foot over the window ledge—half in, half out. Oliver could see Erin standing just behind Gavin on the landing. They were waiting for him.

Oliver shook his head at his best friend when he caught sight of the Christmas tree.

"Start down without me," he muttered, quickly changing direction. He couldn't leave Grandma Sunday's ornaments here to burn.

"What the fuck are you doing?" Gavin asked, coughing in the thick smoke. "We don't have time."

Glancing over his shoulder, he saw Gavin point toward the stairs that led down to the pub. Oliver followed that direction and saw the first hint of orange light, indicating the fire was making its way upstairs.

"The ornaments," he yelled back, choking on the smoke as well. "Go! Go!"

Gavin shook his head, but Oliver wasn't leaving this pub without the ornaments.

He stared hard at his foster brother. "Go now! Take Erin."

Gavin must have seen the determination written on his face. Unfortunately, he didn't react the way Oliver wanted.

"No!" Oliver yelled when Gavin waved for Erin to start down without them before climbing back over the ledge and into the apartment.

"Gavin, Ollie!" Erin cried from the window as Gavin ran over to Oliver, the two of them frantically trying to find the ornaments in the dim lighting.

"Where the fuck are they?" Gavin said.

They were both coughing hard now, the air a thick cloud of smoke. Seeing was hard, breathing harder.

"Here!" Gavin said, holding up two ornaments he'd found.

Oliver's eyes watered and burned, his chest tight from lack of oxygen.

Fuck yeah—he had the other two. "Let's go!"

He and Gavin raced to the fire escape. Erin was halfway down, only starting her descent when she saw them heading toward her. He'd give her hell later for not getting to safety immediately, but that would have to wait until he could breathe again. Right now, he was coughing so hard, he was afraid he'd drop the damn ornaments he could now admit he'd stupidly risked his life and Gavin's to save.

They rounded the side of the building as a police car took the corner way too fucking fast, squealing its tires, the siren piercing the night. Slamming on the brakes and throwing the car in park, Aaron emerged from the cruiser, clearly ready to race into the burning building.

"Aaron!" Oliver yelled, drawing his uncle's attention as they ran across the street to him.

"Call came through dispatch. I wasn't far away," Aaron said. "Thank God you three got out! No one else—"

"No. No one," Oliver said, his voice tight, throat inflamed from the smoke. Speaking was painful. "Pub's been closed for hours."

A fire truck pulled up in front of the pub, the firefighters jumping down and rushing around to unroll the hoses.

Glass shattered, and Oliver turned at the sound. He saw flames shooting out the front of the pub through the hole where the large plate glass window proudly bearing the name Pat's Irish Pub used to be.

"Fuck," Gavin said, coughing hard. "Jesus. *Fuck!*"

Aaron put a comforting hand on Gavin's shoulder, and then Oliver's, as the two of them continued to gasp for air, their struggles for deep breaths broken up by hard, rib-rattling coughs.

Oliver's gaze took in the entire building, and while the flames weren't visible on the top two floors yet, he knew there would be no saving them if the firefighters didn't get the hoses hooked up to the hydrant, the water pumping, and the blaze under control quickly.

As it was, the pub and Sunday's Side were already engulfed in fire, and there was no doubt they couldn't be saved.

He glanced to his side as Gavin continued to cough deeply. They'd both taken in too much smoke. "I'm sorry," he murmured, unsure if his foster brother even heard him as more fire trucks and police cars arrived, Landon and Miguel climbing out of one of the cars and racing over to them.

"Thank God!" Miguel said, enveloping Erin in a big hug. "When we heard...all I could think..."

"We're okay," Erin said, her voice muffled against Miguel's uniform.

"Layla already called me," Miguel said. "The alarm sent an alert to Finn's phone. They're on their way here. Let me call, tell her you're..." Miguel, still frazzled and upset, released Erin and pulled out his phone, calling his girlfriend. Oliver overheard him telling Layla that they'd all gotten out.

It was just as he thought. Most of his family would be here soon. Finn's alarm system included an app, and after a long after-noon—which had been painful at the time but funny afterwards when they retold the story—they'd managed to teach the older generation how to download and use it.

Gavin succumbed to another coughing fit.

"Ambulance on the way," Landon said.

"Don't need one," Gavin rasped.

Oliver wanted to argue with his foster brother. Then he started coughing as well. But there was no way in hell he was going to the hospital. No way he was leaving until the fire was out.

Landon ignored Gavin. "EMTs will check you both out. Smoke inhalation is no joke and it sounds like you two sucked in a lot." Then he walked to the end of the street to stand next to Miguel, who was directing traffic—not that there was much at this time of night. Mainly just the rescue vehicles.

Actually, Oliver wasn't even sure this classified as night anymore. It was after four a.m. Morning.

Oliver looked at the two ornaments still clasped in his hands, then glanced at Gavin, overwhelmed by guilt.

"Gavin—" he started.

Gavin cut him off. "You were right to save them."

"You shouldn't have come—"

"Stop." Gavin's face was streaked with lines of black soot caused by the combination of smoke and watering eyes. "I go where you go, brother. Always."

Oliver didn't know how to reply to that. He probably couldn't if he tried. His throat was no longer tight, it was closed. Completely blocked by tears he couldn't shed.

Or shock. Maybe this was shock.

More cars pulled up, and Oliver saw Layla emerge from a passenger seat. Erin cried out and left his side, running to her cousin, the two of them hugging tightly. Finn stood next to them, his gaze glued to the pub.

Padraig, who had an apartment a few blocks away, sprinted down the sidewalk. His hair was a mess, his shoes untied. He hadn't even bothered to dress or put on a coat, racing to the pub in his pajamas.

"Jesus," he said as he came to a halt next to Oliver. He pulled Oliver into his arms, then reached over to include Gavin in the bear hug. "Jesus," he said again as he released them. "I thought. I...fuck..."

Then he, like Finn, turned to look at the building, his expression one of total devastation. "Oh fuck."

Oliver swallowed hard, the act causing him to cough once more.

"No no no nooooo! God, no!"

Oliver turned at the sound of Riley's voice, and the tears he'd managed to keep at bay so far started to fall when he saw her and Pop Pop walking down the sidewalk toward them. Riley raced up to them, tears streaming down her face. "Ollie!" she said, kissing him on the cheek. "Gavin." She gave Gavin the same kiss, then dashed over to Aaron, who'd seen her arrive. She ran straight into her husband's arms, trembling, crying.

"You shouldn't be here, Pop Pop," Padraig said as their grandfather stopped next to them.

"This is exactly where I should be." Like Padraig before him, Pop Pop gripped Oliver's upper arm and Gavin's, twisting both so he could look at them.

"You're both okay?" Pop Pop asked, his eyes filled with concern.

He and Gavin both nodded, and it occurred to Oliver that he wasn't the only one fighting off some pretty strong emotions. Gavin looked just as distraught, the seriousness of what they'd just escaped only now dawning on them.

"You're sure? Not lying to me?" Pop Pop continued to look them up and down as if unwilling to take them at their word, then he reached up, cupping Oliver's cheek.

"I'm sure," Oliver croaked.

Pop Pop pierced Gavin with a look.

"I'm fine," Gavin reassured Pop Pop.

"Erin?" Pop Pop asked.

Gavin pointed farther down the block. "There with Layla. She's fine too."

"I was so afraid. When Riley woke me up, when she said..." Pop Pop stopped and, for the first time, his grandfather turned to look at the pub, the flames reflected in his misty eyes.

Pop Pop had spent the majority of his life within the walls of that building, immigrating from Ireland when he was in his twenties with his bride, Sunday. He'd raised his family, run the pub and the restaurant, sat by his wife's side as cancer consumed her, and celebrated countless birthdays, holidays, graduations, weddings, and the birth of babies here.

An entire life—contained within four walls. Four walls now scorched by flames and smoke, gutted by the fire still raging within.

Oliver squeezed his eyes closed tightly, trying to block out the broken expression on Pop Pop's face. It had been a brief look; his grandfather—one of the strongest men he'd ever known—had schooled his features quickly. Oliver suspected he was probably the only one who'd seen that split second of raw emotion, of unspeakable pain.

When Oliver opened his eyes again, he had to look away from Pop Pop before he fell completely apart, but there was no escape. Aunt Keira and Uncle Ewan had arrived. The two of them managed Sunday's Side, the restaurant where Riley was the cook. The three siblings had worked together for decades, practically their whole lives.

Ewan watched the blaze, his eyes lined with pain, his arms wrapped tightly around Keira and Riley. He tucked them close as his sisters both quietly cried against his chest. "It's okay," Ewan murmured to them over and over. "It's okay."

The image shattered Oliver's heart into a million pieces.

Tris, who ran the pub side with his son, Padraig, arrived next. He stopped beside Padraig, and the two of them wrapped their arms around each other's shoulders, neither looking away from their beloved pub, watching as the flames reduced everything inside to ash.

"I called Colm on the way here," Tris said to Padraig. "He's on his way, son."

Oliver was glad to hear that. Padraig had suffered so much loss in the last few years. He was only just now starting to move on after Mia's death. Oliver was afraid to consider what this might do to his beloved cousin. Padraig would need the support of his twin brother, Colm, if the outright desolation on his face was anything to go by.

The firefighters continued to fight the blaze for what felt like hours, though realistically, Oliver doubted much more than an hour had passed since they'd escaped the pub.

The EMTs looked over him and Gavin briefly, but both of them refused to go to the hospital, despite his mother's insistence. Lauren and his two dads had arrived later than the others. Because they didn't work at the pub, they didn't have the alarm system app on their phones. Instead, they'd found out about the fire after a call from Aaron.

The EMTs offered them blankets, reminding Oliver that he, Gavin, and Erin were decidedly underdressed for the winter weather. Hell, they were all barefoot. Seemed weird to him that he couldn't even feel the cold.

More and more of the family began to arrive, all of them in various states of dress as they'd been pulled from their beds, called by loved ones. Shoulder to shoulder, they stood across the street, watching, until at last, the water was shut off and the fire-fighters began to stow their equipment.

"It's out," Aaron said, crossing the street to them after a brief chat with the fire chief. "Most of the fire was contained to the first floor. There was...a substantial amount of damage." Aaron stumbled to explain, and it was clear he didn't want to say that the pub and the restaurant had been completely destroyed. "There's water and smoke damage to the upper floors. Most everything up there is...a total loss as well."

"How did it start?" Ewan asked.

Aaron shrugged. "All they can tell right now is it started in the kitchen. The fire inspector will come by in the morning." Aaron seemed to realize it was already morning, dawn breaking, and corrected himself. "In a few hours to take a look."

Riley gasped. "The kitchen. Pop—" Riley's voice broke as she wrapped her arm around her father's waist. "It's my fault."

"What?" Pop Pop asked.

Riley and Padraig exchanged a glance, and Gavin cursed beside Oliver.

"Shit. The outlet?" Gavin said.

"What outlet?" Oliver asked.

"One of the outlets in the kitchen stopped working this week. I kept breaking the circuit, overloading the other outlets." Riley looked at Gavin. "I wish I'd..."

"No. Don't. I should have insisted on looking at it Tuesday night," Gavin said quietly.

Riley shook her head. "My fault. I told you it could wait until the weekend."

"It's no one's fault," Pop Pop said.

Riley refused to believe that. "You're wrong. God. I can't believe this! Can't believe I fucked up so—"

"Language, Riley," Pop Pop said, cupping Riley's face and giving her a gentle smile. His grandfather had said that word to all of them more times than any of them could count, not that it had done a damn bit of good when it came to curbing their love of curse words.

"But, Pop—" Riley started, the joke missing its mark.

"I won't hear another word from you, young lady," Pop Pop said in a stern tone Oliver had only heard a handful of times in his life.

Riley nodded, though it was clear she wouldn't stop blaming herself. Oliver hated seeing the pain, the guilt in her eyes.

Apparently, Aaron didn't like it either. He put his arm around his wife and kissed the top of her head. "It's not your fault, Riley. Let it go, sweetheart. It's going to be okay."

Riley twisted and buried her face in her husband's chest, holding on to him tightly.

Pop Pop stepped off the curb and took a couple steps toward the pub. Oliver wondered if he was trying to get a closer look, and he was ready to intervene before his grandfather got too near. Not only was it unsafe, but he didn't want Pop Pop to see just how bad it was. It looked horrible enough from this side of the street.

However, Pop Pop surprised him when he turned his back to the pub, facing all of them, still huddled close together.

"Everything that matters," Pop Pop said, his voice surprisingly strong as he held his arms out, gesturing to all of them, "is on this side of the street. *Everything.*"

Oliver looked around and saw his beloved family standing

side by side, healthy, whole, alive. Erin and Gavin flanked him, and when he considered how much worse this could have been if they hadn't been able to get out, if he'd lost one or both of them...Pop Pop was right.

"We'll rebuild it, Pop," Oliver's dad, Sean, said, stepping next to his father and placing his hand on his shoulder.

Pop Pop smiled. "Of course we will."

"We'll make it better than before," Uncle Killian added.

"We're going to rearrange our schedule at J and K Construction," Uncle Justin added. "Pat's Pub just moved up to the top of our list of projects."

"My brothers will help too," Layla called out. "Moretti Brothers Restorations. I promise you, they'll be able to make it look exactly the same."

For the first time since waking up to the alarm, the two-ton weight that had been pressing on Oliver's chest began to lift. The Collins family might get knocked down, but damn if they didn't get right the hell back up again.

It was then that Oliver remembered the ornaments. He'd been cupping them in his hands through everything, unwilling to release them. He glanced over at Gavin, who nodded, holding up the two in his hands, aware of where his thoughts had traveled.

The two of them walked over to Pop Pop, palms upright, revealing what they held.

Pop Pop's eyes widened. "Sunday's ornaments."

Riley gasped. "You saved them."

His aunts and uncles crowded closer to look. He and Gavin handed them to Riley, Keira, Ewan, and Tris, who cradled each ornament, as if they were newborn babies.

Oliver's dad, Sean, stepped between him and Gavin, the only Collins sibling who wasn't smiling at the moment. Wrapping his arms around their shoulders, he pulled them out of earshot of the rest of the family. "I'm not sure I like the idea of the two of you stopping to undecorate a Christmas tree in the middle of a fire. What the hell were you thinking?"

"It was my fault," Oliver said. "I ran to the tree to grab them. Gavin tried to stop me."

"Ollie—" Gavin interjected, shaking his head.

"Dammit, Oliver," Dad started. "So not only did you risk your own life, you risked that of your brother's. Where was Erin?"

Oliver sighed. "On the fire escape. Waiting."

"Jesus," Dad said, his jaw suddenly tight.

"He wasn't wrong," Gavin said, drawing Dad's attention to him. "This family lost enough tonight, Sean. It only took us a second to grab the ornaments. If I thought we were in danger, I would have dragged him out of there, ornaments or not. I swear it."

Dad nodded, and a ghost of smile appeared. "When Aaron called and said the pub was on fire, I lost ten years off my life. Even when he said you were both alright, I couldn't relax until I saw you with my own eyes."

Gavin blew out a long, slow breath. "Looks like we're homeless."

Oliver hadn't considered that. Shit. He'd spent the last hour thinking only of what his family had lost. Hadn't spared a thought about himself.

He and Gavin had just lost everything.

Dad glanced over his shoulder at the pub briefly before turning his back on it again as if it was too hard to acknowledge. "I realize we've sort of taken control of your old bedrooms..."

Oliver and Gavin chuckled. *Sort of* was an understatement. His parents had turned Oliver's old bedroom into a home gym, and Gavin's was currently awash in fabric as their mother had taken up quilting and decided she needed a sewing room.

"We still have the guest room, and we can move some furniture around tomorrow...or, damn. It *is* tomorrow. So, later this afternoon. We'll get your rooms back together for you," Dad offered.

"Or," Erin said, "if you'll forgive me for eavesdropping, you guys could come stay with me. I'm out a roommate at the moment and the extra bedroom, Jordan's old room, is fully furnished. I mean...all the furniture was mine to begin with."

Oliver gripped the edges of the blanket draped over Erin's shoulders, using it to pull her closer, as for the first time he began to feel the cold December air. He wrapped her up in his arms, trying to share what little body heat he had left with her. He looked at Gavin over her head, trying to determine what his foster brother thought of her invitation.

While it wouldn't be much different than what they'd been doing over the past year—Erin typically slept over at their apartment a couple nights a week—Oliver couldn't hide how much he liked the idea of the three of them sharing a space full-time.

Gavin's brow was furrowed, a sure sign he was trying to come up with an excuse to say no.

Oliver stared him down, mouthing the word "please," and Gavin rolled his eyes.

Then the lines in Gavin's forehead eased and he gave Oliver a crooked smile. "That's a nice offer, Erin," he said. "If you're sure, I say we give it a try. And if our testosterone gets to be too much, you can always give us the boot."

The shock was wearing off quickly. Oliver reached out and pulled Gavin toward them, the three of them huddling together. He needed them in his arms, needed to feel them close and know they were all safe.

Oliver swallowed hard. "I love you two. God, if anything had..." He couldn't finish his thought.

"We're okay, bro," Gavin murmured. "We're all okay."

Erin sniffled, then lifted her head, nodding. "We're okay," she reiterated with a sad smile.

Oliver let their words sink in and held them even tighter, overwhelmed by the sudden feeling that everything had changed tonight.

Only he wasn't sure if that was a good thing or a bad thing.

❧ 6 ❧

Gavin answered the door, stepping back as Sean walked into Erin's apartment. A week had passed since the fire. In many ways it felt as if someone had died, as he and Oliver tried to work their way through the stages of grief. The first couple of days afterwards had been spent trying to replace everything they'd lost—their wardrobes, phones, IDs, toiletries, and too many other fucking things to count. He'd been to the DMV, the insurance company, as well as making numerous trips to Walmart and Target.

Sean lifted up a huge bag. "Lauren's been at it again. Found a sale online on Levis jeans. I think she bought them out of your size. Ollie's too."

Gavin chuckled as he took the bag. "I think we officially own more clothes now than before the fire," he joked, though deep inside he was touched by the way the Collins family had rallied around him and Oliver, constantly stopping by to bring them everything from hand-me-downs to new clothes to items they "just happened to have extra" of. Though Gavin would bet his last dollar there was no way Aaron just happened to have two "extra" expensive electric razors laying around his house.

"Where are the other two?" Sean asked, following Gavin to

the kitchen. He nodded when Gavin pulled a cold beer from the fridge, taking it with a quick thanks. Gavin helped himself to one as well. "Erin's at work, though she should be home soon, and Oliver took off after we left the work site to check on Pop Pop, to see how he's doing. I'm supposed to be getting dinner ready. It's my night to cook. Obviously, I'm failing at that."

Sean looked around at the kitchen, chuckling as he acknowledged the fact that absolutely nothing was on the stove. He shrugged and said, "So order pizza."

Gavin dismissed the idea. He'd promised to make a meal. Pizza felt like cheating.

The two of them grabbed a seat at the small table in Erin's kitchen. Gavin had initially had some reservations about moving in here with Erin and Oliver, but he had to admit, the three of them had fallen into their new living arrangements quite easily.

Sean leaned back in the chair. "Actually, I was hoping to get you to myself. I've been meaning to talk to you, but between the fire and all the rebuilding plans going on at work, it's been tough to steal you away."

"What's going on?"

Sean took a long swig of his beer, and Gavin got the sense that whatever his foster dad wanted to say, he wasn't finding it easy. "Aaron said he told you about your mom getting out of the psych hospital."

Gavin nodded, somewhat surprised to learn that Sean knew. He wondered if he was upset with Gavin for not telling him himself.

Of course, in his defense, he'd been so busy this past week, he hadn't had time to give his mother's release more than a passing thought or two. He still hadn't even told Oliver that she was walking around a free woman.

"She called the house last Friday afternoon. Day of the fire. Spoke to Lauren."

Gavin wasn't sure what he'd expected Sean to say, but it sure as fuck wasn't that. "Why would she do that?"

"She's had our names for years, knew that we took you in after she was committed."

"She's looking for me." Gavin wasn't sure why, but the thought of his mother calling and talking to Lauren upset him more than he would have thought. He never—*never*—wanted his mother anywhere near Sean, Lauren, or Chad.

Sean nodded. "And I can see by the look on your face that pisses you off. I figured as much, but, well, your mom—Lauren," Sean clarified.

"Lauren *is* my mom," he admitted softly. Gavin was always touched when Sean and Chad referred to themselves as his dads and Lauren his mom. God knew that was what he considered them, even if he'd never been able to call them by those names.

It was still difficult for him to understand, to accept, their unconditional love. Not that they ever stopped trying to get him there.

Sean reached over and patted his hand. "Maybe one day you'll give those mom and dad titles a spin. I mean, I don't mind you calling me Sean, but, well...Dad has a nice ring to it too. Should have made that offer a long time ago, but..."

"But I never gave you the chance," Gavin finished for him. "I know I was a giant pain in the ass during those early years, pretending like I didn't give a shit about any of you, making your lives hell. Can't believe you didn't kick me to the curb."

Sean was the most fun-loving of Gavin's three foster parents, while Lauren and Chad, both psychologists, were more serious. So it was strange to look at Sean now and not see that permanent smile on his face. "We were never going to send you away, Gavin. That's not what family does. We love each other through all of it—the good and the bad times. When you walked into our house that first time with Margie, that badass smirk on your face, I knew in an instant you were meant to be my son. Never saw a stronger kid. The shit your mom put you through would have broken a lesser man. Hell, it would have broken *me*. But not you. Jesus, son. How you grew up in the midst of all that pain and uncertainty with that big heart of yours still intact, I'll never know."

Gavin swallowed hard, afraid to speak, knowing it would give away just how close he was to the verge of tears.

"So I'm just saying...I know you're a grown-ass man now, but if you want to drop the Sean thing and move over to Dad...that works for me. Just know, if you call me that, you have to call Chad Dad too. He's a jealous son of a bitch."

Gavin laughed. There wasn't a jealous bone in Chad's body, and Sean knew it, just as he knew exactly how to lighten the mood with a joke. He'd known for years Sean and Chad considered him their son. Maybe they didn't share the same blood, but that didn't matter to either of them.

When Gavin thought about all the things Sean had given him over the years—both material and emotional—none of it made him as happy as this offer.

"We planned to tell you about the call last weekend, but then...with the fire..."

"It's okay."

"Lauren didn't give your mother your number. She refused to tell her where you were until we talked to you. You want to see her?"

Gavin hesitated, unsure how to answer. He'd known this was coming, knew she would seek him out, that she would want to see him. But his feelings about that reunion were just as fucked up as they'd been last week. Hell, maybe more so. This week, after the fire, he'd been running on fumes, his emotions raw.

Finally, he shook his head. "Not yet."

Lauren and Chad had given him books about dealing with childhood abuse, in addition to talking to him about his feelings toward his mother. In the past few years, as he'd gotten older, Lauren had begun to share some online information about what it meant to live with a sociopath.

Every single description had been textbook of the life he'd lived, of his mother's pathology—her lack of empathy, her disregard for right and wrong, her aggression, her ability to manipulate him to get what she wanted. If there'd been a checkbox next to each description, he could have ticked off every single one.

And it was that information that had him hesitating to schedule a reunion. Regardless of the fact he now understood why she did the things she did, he also knew *himself*. Knew his personality—his compulsion to take care of someone he loved—didn't mesh with hers. Not at all.

Not to mention, he was still eaten up with guilt for not going to visit her. Whether that feeling was right or wrong didn't matter. It was still there. Always in the back of his mind.

He'd never completely opened up to his foster parents, never told them everything that had happened to him, but he'd always listened to them, to their reassurances that he wasn't alone, that he was stronger than the things he'd suffered. He'd soaked in their words, drank them down like a man dying of thirst.

Gavin realized that unlike him, most kids never got a clean slate, a chance to see parenting from a different perspective. While some might consider fifteen too old to save a kid, Gavin *had* been saved. Sean, Lauren, and Chad had taught him to love —not only others, but himself as well.

"Fine. If she calls back, we'll tell her you're not ready. But, Gavin, if she's determined to find you..."

"It won't be that hard. I'm still in Baltimore, working with you, living with Ollie. It's okay. If she finds me, I'll deal with it."

Sean reached over and placed his large, strong hand on Gavin's shoulder. "I'm proud of the man you've become."

Gavin gave him a wobbly smile. "Thanks." It was on the tip of his tongue to add Dad, but the word got stuck in his throat.

They stood up at the same time, Sean pulling him close for the quintessential man hug, giving him two hard slaps on the back.

"Well, I'm heading home. Layla's brothers are coming down from Philly on Monday to look at the pub."

In addition to trying to replace all the shit they'd lost, he and

Oliver had spent the better part of the last three days with Sean, Justin, Killian, and a huge construction crew, gutting the pub and restaurant, reinforcing the structure, pulling out all the burned furniture, shoveling tons of soot and ash, taking the interior down to bare beams. There was still a lot of work to do, but with each passing day, he felt more and more certain they could bring the place back to life.

"What time's the meeting?" Gavin asked. "Wouldn't mind stopping in to say hello to those guys."

Over the course of the past two years, the Moretti brothers had made more than a few trips to Baltimore—they really were overprotective when it came to Layla and Erin—and as such, they'd been absorbed into the Collins clan. He'd thrown back quite a few pints with Tony, Joe, Luca, and Gio in the pub, and he was grateful for their willingness to help restore it.

"Around ten o'clock. We've been pulling together as many pictures of the pub and Sunday's Side as we can find, to help them once our construction crew puts the bones of the place back together. At the rate we've been going, we can start drywalling in a couple of weeks. Tony assures us they can make it look exactly the same."

"That's good. Riley doing okay?"

Sean shrugged. "She's been better. She's still blaming herself. I was hoping the fire inspector would come back with something other than electrical fire, but..."

"I knew what caused it the second Riley mentioned that outlet. I'm so sorry I didn't..."

"Don't you start too. No one is to blame. It was an accident caused by old as shit wiring. If it hadn't started behind the walls, the sprinkler system might have knocked it down, but...oh fuck it. Lots of buts that don't change a damn thing. We're rebuilding it and it'll be better than ever. That's all that matters."

Gavin nodded, letting Sean's words sink in. He'd had a hard time shaking off his own guilt over his part in not preventing the fire, but Sean was right. It was time to look ahead instead of crying over what-ifs.

"Guess I should start dinner."

Sean shook his head. "Order pizza."

"I promised—"

"Dammit, Gavin. You had two pretty big life-altering shocks these last couple of weeks. Take the Boy Scout hat off for a night and give yourself a break."

Gavin rolled his eyes good-naturedly. "Fine." His foster family had dubbed him the Boy Scout, proclaiming the caregiver gene ran strong inside him. He'd never bothered to tell him he was pretty sure it wasn't nature but nurture that had created his need to take care of others.

He and Sean said their goodbyes, and Gavin walked back to the refrigerator, determined to figure out dinner. He'd just about convinced himself pizza really *was* his best bet—he was in no mood to cook—when Erin got home.

"Guys?" she called out.

"In here," Gavin replied.

Erin appeared at the entrance to the kitchen. "Hey," she said tiredly, looking around. "Ollie not home yet?"

Gavin shook his head. "Went to visit his Pop Pop. Long day?"

She sighed heavily. "Yeah. I've had better. You haven't started dinner yet, have you?"

He gave her a guilty grin. "I was going to suggest we order pizza." Then he realized she had a grocery bag in her hand. "But...you have something else in mind?" He gestured toward the bag.

"Yes. I need comfort food. My mom's comfort food." She walked into the kitchen and started unloading the groceries. "Homemade lasagna."

"Damn. That sounds good. But I feel bad. You cooked last night."

She pierced him with a haughty glare. "Oh, I'm not cooking alone. You've just be recruited as my kitchen help. And you're going to clean up the mess. I'm warning you now...it will be substantial."

He chuckled and saluted. "Fine. Tell me what to do."

She tossed the cellophane-wrapped package of mushrooms at him. "Wash and slice those for me. And never," she waved a box of lasagna noodles in the air, "tell my mother I used store noodles in her recipe."

Gavin nodded solemnly. "I'll take your secret to the grave."

The two of them worked in silence for a few minutes as he chopped the vegetables she kept tossing his way, while she assembled and cooked the sauce.

"Want to talk about work?" he asked, when it was clear she wasn't going to broach the subject on her own. It was rare for him to have to prod her for a story, which told him today really *had* been rough on her.

She lifted one shoulder, staring intently at the sauce. "A little girl was brought to the E.R. in an ambulance. She'd been riding her bike. Hit by a car." The story was coming out choppy. "It was bad. Really bad." Her voice broke.

"Is she okay?" Gavin asked quietly.

"It's still touch and go. Brain trauma. The thing is...it was her brother."

"What?"

"Her older brother had just gotten his driver's license. He didn't see her. He was the one who hit her."

"Fuck," Gavin muttered.

"Yeah. Spent the afternoon watching that poor mother fearing for her daughter's life while consoling her son. I...I just don't know how she was holding it together like that. She was... so strong. I think if I'd been her, I would have been in a fetal position in the corner."

"I doubt that," Gavin said, stepping next to her, putting his arm around her shoulders. "You do one of the toughest jobs there is, Erin. Constantly surrounded by pain, suffering, even death. And you always do it with a compassion, a kindness, a strength most people will never possess." He kissed the top of her head. "You're an amazing person."

She looked up at him, smiling, though her lashes were wet with unshed tears. "Thank you. God..." She wiped at her eyes. "You always know exactly what to say to make me feel better."

"The little girl will be fine. I'm sure of it."

Erin nodded, letting his reassurance soak in. "Yeah. She will."

She picked up the heavy wooden spoon to stir the sauce once more but lost her grip. It dropped into the pan, splashing sauce all over one of his new white shirts. "Oh my God, Gavin! I'm so sorry. Here." She reached for the hem of his shirt and started to lift it before he realized her intent. "Give it to me. I'll soak it right away."

Gavin stepped back, quickly tugging the material back down.

Erin looked at him, confused. "We have to wash the sauce out immediately so it doesn't stain."

"It's okay," he said, his fingers tight around the hem of the shirt, holding it down when she reached out once more, determined to take it off him.

Her brow was furrowed for just a moment or two before he saw realization dawn. Erin had never seen him without his shirt —and she was only just now comprehending that.

"Gavin," she started, her confusion turning to concern. Which meant he was doing a piss-poor job of shielding his panic.

"I'll go change. I have some stain stuff I can use."

He started to leave, but Erin blocked his path. "Take off your shirt."

He frowned. "No."

"Why not?"

"What?"

She crossed her arms and repeated herself slowly. "Why. Not?"

He wondered if she hadn't had such a shitty day, if her emotions hadn't already been too close to the surface, if she would have pushed him. Then he decided she would. She had a habit of pushing, and for some reason he let her get away with it, when with others, he pushed back harder and walked away.

"Let it go, Erin," he said, adopting a tone that would have warned off most people.

"Are you hurt?" she asked, genuine apprehension in her gaze.

"No." He ran his hand through his hair. "Fuck. No. I'm fine." Then, because he didn't know what else to say, he pointed at her shirt. "You got sauce on you too."

She glanced down at her top—she was still in her scrubs—and sighed. "So I do." Holding his gaze, she reached down and pulled her top off, her hair falling over her bare shoulders as she stood before him in just her bra.

It belatedly occurred to him that this was the second time in a week he'd seen her in some state of undress. It hadn't registered until just this minute that she'd been completely naked the night of the fire. That he'd been the one to dress her.

Shouldn't the two of them have felt some sort of unease over that? He didn't. And given the fact she didn't hesitate to take her shirt off now, it was clear she wasn't uncomfortable with it either.

Gavin wasn't sure how to feel about anything these days. He closed his eyes briefly, not opening them until he heard her stepping away, the water of the sink running.

Gavin took two steps toward the door, ready to make a quick, cowardly escape.

She stopped him when she said, "You know, I tell you everything." Her voice was soft and sad. "You're one of the best friends I've ever had. Talking to you always makes me feel better. I hope..." She paused, and Gavin swallowed hard, bracing himself for the rest. "I hope someday you'll trust me enough to let me in."

Gavin gripped the doorframe, fighting to leave as hard as he was fighting to stay. Glancing over his shoulder, he watched Erin scrubbing the stain out of her shirt with a vengeance. She didn't look in his direction when he turned back toward her.

She straightened when he tossed his T-shirt over her head, into the water with hers.

But he gripped her shoulders before she could turn around. She struggled for a second, and he held her tight, stopping her with one word.

"Don't." His tone dark, harsh, even to his own ears.

Erin froze.

"My mother isn't dead."

"What?"

"She didn't die. She was committed...to a psychiatric hospital."

Erin tried to turn around again, but he stopped her again. "No. Don't move."

"Gavin—"

"My mother was brutally raped. That's how she got pregnant with me. I have no idea if...if that attack changed her into the woman I knew. Or if she was always so... She's a sociopath and a drunk, Erin. A mean, abusive one. She started...hurting me when I was six. Not sure what snapped in her at that point, or if she just decided I was suddenly old enough to be her whipping boy."

"Gavin—" she started again.

"When she was drunk or in one of her black rages, she beat me, told me I ruined her life. I was never sure if it was me she was punishing during those times or if...if in her twisted, sick mind, she thought I was the man who'd hurt her. And then, when she was sober, she'd beg for my forgiveness, always promising it was the last time, that she'd get better, swearing she loved me, telling me I was all she had."

Erin stopped trying to turn around. She remained quiet, and if he wasn't standing here with his guts ripped out, he might have been amused by the fact that he'd actually rendered the queen of talkers speechless.

"She never got better."

"Oh God," she breathed, the sound shaky, betraying how close she was to tears.

"I just wanted you to know that, so you'd understand when... you see me."

Erin nodded but didn't try to move. Not until he released his grip on her shoulders and took a step back. Even then, she remained as she was for a second, and he watched as she straightened her spine. He knew her well enough to know she was preparing herself, digging deep to find that strength he'd just told her he admired. Maybe never more so than in this moment.

When she turned around, she kept her eyes on his, and if she'd shed tears as he spoke, she'd gotten them under control now. He held his breath when her gaze lowered.

She didn't say anything as she looked at his chest, at the scars, some hidden behind the tattoos, others still waiting to be concealed.

Erin started to circle him slowly, her eyes missing nothing as she looked at the long, jagged white scar on his arm, evidence of that final blow, the slice of the knife.

She stopped when she stood behind him.

His back was the worst, he knew it. When he was younger, he'd always turned away from his mother, the reaction sheer protective instinct, so his back had taken the brunt of the abuse —the cuts from broken liquor bottles, the cigarette burns. Bruises faded and went away. Cuts and burns left a lasting stain.

He'd always wondered if that had been his mother's intent. If she'd wanted him to have visible proof of just exactly who he belonged to. After all, he couldn't look at himself in the mirror and *not* think of her, every single time his gaze landed on the scars.

Gavin braced himself in case Erin reached out to touch him, holding himself still as stone. Oliver was the only one who'd ever touched his scars, and it was taking everything he had not to walk away from her, out of this room.

When she completed her circle, she stopped in front of him, her hands still by her side.

"Thank you for showing me. For trusting me," she whispered.

He nodded, unable to speak.

The softness in her eyes turned to what he'd come to know as pure Moretti steel when she added, "And if I ever meet your mother, I'm ripping every fucking hair out of her scalp. And then I'm gonna get serious."

Gavin wasn't sure what he'd expected her to say, but it wasn't that, and he couldn't hold back the loud bark of laughter. Erin didn't share his mirth, her anger over his scars too new, too hot. He'd had a lifetime to look at them, so it was easier for him.

He reached out and grabbed her, pulled her into his arms for a hug, no longer worried about her touching him. When she wrapped her arms around his, her fingers brushing over the scars, he waited for the horror to sink in. It didn't.

Instead, all he felt was her softness, her warmth, and a comfort he'd never experienced before. "Gotta admit. I'm sort of tempted to introduce you to her now," he joked, shocking himself with his response.

Erin, like Oliver, always knew exactly how to soothe his hurts, to make him feel almost normal in the face of something that was so fucking abnormal. She lifted her head to look at him, even as they remained connected, skin to skin, but she didn't say anything. She didn't need to. The compassion in her eyes warmed him all the way to the bone and stirred something in his heart he couldn't recognize, couldn't define at first.

Then he figured it out. Erin had done it. Broken through the last of his barriers. He couldn't believe how fucking good it felt.

"Come on," he said, clearing his throat in an attempt to hide the thickness in his voice. "Let's grab clean shirts and finish this lasagna. I'm starving."

❦

AN HOUR LATER, HE SAT AT THE KITCHEN TABLE WITH ERIN and Oliver, the three of them putting a serious dent in the homemade lasagna. After changing shirts, he and Erin had returned to the kitchen, and while things between them were as easy as always, there was also a new...layer...to their relationship. It was as if their friendship had deepened in those few minutes, pulling them even closer. Oliver was the only other person Gavin had ever let so far in, and a small part of him kept waiting for that moment when regret over showing her his back kicked in.

It hadn't hit yet. Maybe it wouldn't.

"How's your Pop Pop doing?" Gavin asked.

Oliver shrugged. "Hanging in there. The man is stronger than me, that's for damn sure. He showed me where they hung Grandma Sunday's ornaments on the tree at Riley and Aaron's house. It felt...weird."

"Yeah. Christmas is going to be different this year." Gavin's first true Christmas had been spent with the Collins family the year he'd come to live with them. The entire family celebrated at the pub because no one's house was big enough to hold them all. Gavin could recall feeling completely overwhelmed, hugging a wall near the back of the room as he took it all in. He'd admitted to Oliver a few years later that until he'd seen a Collins Christmas, he'd always thought holiday movies were full of shit, pure fiction, certain that no one did the big tree, the carol singing, and all the hugging and presents. He and his mother typically went to the shelter for a free meal, then came home, carrying on as if it was any other day.

Oliver wiped his mouth with his napkin. "Caitlyn insists there's plenty of room for all of us to celebrate at her new house."

"She's not wrong," Gavin said. "We could have put two of the pubs in that mansion of hers."

Oliver's oldest cousin, Caitlyn, had married billionaire, Lucas Whiting. They'd had their first child last spring, at which point Lucas insisted they needed a bigger house. Caitlyn still joked about the enormity of the house he'd found for them, proclaiming they could both roam around for weeks and never find each other.

Lucas said he wanted to make sure there was plenty of room for their seven kids, while Caitlyn reminded him that they were stopping at two. The Collins family had a wager going over whether or not Caitlyn would hold firm to that number, the majority of the bets in favor of Lucas coming out on top.

Their first child, a little girl named Gretchen, already had her father wrapped around her finger, and Lucas was ready to start working on baby number two. For a man who'd spent the first thirty-nine years of his life amassing wealth and determined to hold on to his bachelor status, Lucas had done a complete one-eighty now, declaring there was nothing like life as a family man.

"It'll only be for one year. By this time next year, we'll be back in the pub. Back in the apartment above," Oliver said.

Gavin nodded but not necessarily because he agreed. Now that Erin and Oliver had taken the leap and moved in with each other, he couldn't see them going back to the way things were.

Which would, once again, thrust him into the position of odd man out.

After dinner, they cleaned up the dishes and watched the hockey game on TV, he and Oliver pissed off when the Caps lost to the Bruins in double overtime.

"That's me for the night," Gavin said, standing up and stretching. "I'm worn out."

"Yeah, we won't be too far behind you," Oliver said.

"Night, Gavin," Erin said, smiling at him just the same as always. He was relieved she wasn't suddenly viewing him with pity. That would have killed him.

Then, he wondered briefly if she would tell Oliver what had happened in the kitchen. It didn't matter one way or the other. If she didn't, he would. And then he'd tell the two of them about his mother being released from the psychiatric hospital. He still hadn't dropped that bomb, but tonight didn't feel like the right time, considering he'd only just told Erin she wasn't dead.

Gavin trudged down the hall to his room. Oliver and Erin shared her bedroom. Climbing into bed, the exhaustion he'd felt in the living room vanished as he tossed and turned restlessly. It was annoying because he truly couldn't put his finger on what exactly was wrong with him. Instead, his mind leapt from one thing to the next, never landing on anything for long.

For the last hour, the apartment had been quiet. Obviously, Oliver and Erin had gone to bed.

Gavin stood up and quietly opened the door to his room, prepared to raid the fridge. Maybe a midnight snack would help settle him down.

Erin's apartment had an open plan, the doorway to the kitchen to the left, while the living room and dining room were one big space.

He'd just reached the door to the kitchen when a noise— heavy breathing and a low moan—captured his attention and he looked toward the couch.

He froze when he saw Erin, naked, on top of Oliver. Riding him.

Gavin stood there for several minutes, waging an internal war with himself. He should turn around and go back to his room. That was the sane, rational, respectful thing to do.

However, the voyeuristic side was winning.

Big-time.

Erin's hands were on Oliver's bare chest, her fingers stroking his pecs as she slowly rose and fell. Oliver's hands were on her breasts and he was plumping them, toying with her nipples, which were hard, erect.

"Lean down," Oliver said, his voice deep, sexy. "I want to taste you."

Erin shifted until her breasts were just above Oliver's waiting mouth. Gavin watched his best friend suck one of her nipples, his cock stirring at the sound of Erin's aroused groan.

"God, Ollie," she whispered. "So good."

Oliver continued to suck on her tit as one hand stroked down her side, settling on her hip.

"Suck harder," Erin urged.

Oliver obviously found the sweet spot, his rough suction spurring Erin to ride him faster. Oliver released her nipple with a pop as Erin pushed herself upright again.

"So deep," she murmured. "You're so deep inside me."

"You feel so good, sweet girl."

Sweet girl.

Gavin reached down and ran his hand over his erection. He'd gone rock hard the second Oliver had sucked Erin's nipple into his mouth.

He shouldn't be here.

God, he shouldn't be here.

But he couldn't look away. He stroked himself as he watched them.

No.

Not them.

Her.

Erin's body was lifting and falling, her breasts bouncing, as Oliver's large hands spanned her tiny waist. They fit together perfectly. He'd never seen a naked woman, never felt that desire. Every lover in his past had been male, all his porn man on man, but there was no denying she was gorgeous, sexy.

Then he recalled her hug earlier, how soft her skin and her body had felt. Men were built harder, rougher. She'd felt like a silk pillow, one he wanted to stroke with his fingertips, to rub his cheek against, nestle close to.

"Say it, Erin," Oliver urged. "Need to hear, to know…"

"God. Ollie." Erin's breathing grew more rapid, then it stuttered for a moment as her eyes drifted closed. She threw her head back as pleasure consumed her. Then she cried out the last thing he'd ever expected to hear. "Gavin."

His heart stopped beating as he fought to believe what he'd heard.

Had she really said his name?

He couldn't lower his gaze, couldn't look away as she came. He'd never seen anything so…beautiful.

He pressed on his cock harder, suddenly aware he was close to coming himself.

Gavin took a step back, but froze when Oliver groaned, his own climax coming to claim him.

Gavin turned his attention to Oliver's face and watched as his hips lurched upwards, his back arching as he came inside her.

Fuck.

Gavin returned to his room as quickly, as quietly as he could. Closing the door behind him, he pushed his sweatpants down, gripped his cock, and jerked it roughly, fantasizing about what he'd just witnessed.

Less than a dozen strokes later and he was coming, cupping the head of his dick to catch as much of the come as he could.

He leaned against the door, his strength suddenly zapped. His heart was racing, his eyes clenched shut tightly. He remained there for several minutes, trying to come to grips with what he'd just done.

With what had happened.

And he suddenly understood that sleep was going to continue to elude him.

Because it wasn't Oliver's face he'd just imagined as he jerked himself to completion.

It was Erin's.

¾ 7 ¾

Oliver lifted his head from the pillow, propping himself up on his elbow when Erin sat on the edge of the mattress to put her shoes on.

"Sorry," she said softly. "Didn't mean to wake you."

He waved away her apology. "Wanted to kiss you goodbye anyway. What time do you get off?"

"My shift is over at five, so I'll be here for dinner."

He nodded. "Okay. Gavin and I will hit the store later on and figure out something to make."

She leaned toward him and gave him a quick kiss. "You all are spoiling me. Grocery shopping, cooking, cleaning. Keep this up and I'll never let you leave."

Oliver winked at her. "That's sort of the point."

Erin shook her head. "You're incorrigible."

She had confided in him last night, after Gavin went to bed, that he'd shown her his scars. She'd cried quietly, shaken by the memory, angry at Gavin's mother and devastated to learn that he'd suffered so much pain as a child. She'd known his childhood had been rough, but hearing it and seeing the proof were two different things. Oliver knew that from experience.

Oliver had consoled her, holding her close for a long time. Once she'd pulled herself together, she'd asked him to make love to her. Of course, in the end, she'd made love to *him*, pushing him to his back on the couch and climbing on top. Typically, he took the lead in the bedroom, but he'd gotten a sense that she wanted to call the shots, taking what she needed to wipe away the sad feelings.

Oliver sat up and reached out, pulling her to him for a longer kiss, pressing her lips open and tasting the toothpaste on her breath.

After they'd come last night, they had dragged themselves to bed, both of them still feeling a bit raw. He'd enveloped her in his arms and she'd fallen asleep quickly. It had taken Oliver a lot longer, something weighing heavy on his mind.

When he broke the kiss, he whispered, "He watched us last night."

Erin's silence confirmed his suspicions.

"You knew that, didn't you?"

She nodded. "Yeah. I knew he was there. I...God... What does it say about me that knowing he was watching us totally turned me on?"

"It says you're perfect for me," he joked.

Erin punched his shoulder playfully. "Kinky bastard."

Oliver laughed for a moment but sobered up quickly. "You want it, don't you? The three of us. You're falling for him."

She didn't answer right away. She didn't need to.

"Erin," he prodded.

"I love *you*, Ollie." There was no mistaking the panic—and maybe guilt—in her tone.

He gave her a grin. Sometimes he forgot that most of the world didn't grow up like he did. "Your feelings for Gavin don't negate how you feel about me." He pointed at himself. "Three parents...wildly in love with each other, remember? You can love me *and* Gavin. I think you already do."

"He's easy to love," she admitted. "You both are. But it

doesn't matter how I feel or what we want. He doesn't want...me."

"Sweet girl," he said softly.

She shook her head. "No. You and I both know it wasn't me he was looking at last night. It was you."

Oliver heard the note of dejection in her voice. Pulling her close, he hugged her tightly, kissing her once more as he cupped her cheeks, then lowering his hands to touch her breasts, tempted to wipe the bad feelings away the same way he had last night...with sex.

It probably wasn't the most mature thing to do, but morning wood was a fact of life.

She groaned when he pinched her nipples through her shirt and bra, then broke off the kiss. "Dammit, Ollie, you're making me horny. And I can't be horny. I have to go right now or I'm going to be late."

He chuckled and released her.

Reluctantly.

"Fine. Rain check for later though."

She stood up, bending over for one last quick kiss. "Damn right."

He listened as she walked down the hall, and a few minutes later, he heard the apartment door close behind her. He dropped back onto the bed, debating whether or not to treat himself to another hour of sleep or if he should just go ahead and get up. Saturday was typically his "get shit done" day, when he did the laundry, shopping, and housecleaning. He preferred it that way because that left his Sundays free for just generally being lazy and fucking around.

"Screw it," he murmured. He was already awake, so he decided to get up.

Rising, he dressed and then grabbed the full laundry basket.

He'd just put a load in the washer when he heard Gavin coming out of his room.

"Morning," Gavin said, clearing the sleep out of his throat. "You're up early."

Oliver nodded. "Yeah. Got up with Erin."

"She gone already?" Gavin asked, looking around.

"Yep. Won't be back until five, so I told her we'd fix dinner."

"Um. Yeah. That's cool."

Oliver wasn't sure what to make of the look on his friend's face, trying to decide if Gavin was uncomfortable about Erin seeing the scars or if he was bothered by what he'd seen them doing on the couch.

"Breakfast?" Gavin asked.

"Sure." The two of them ventured to the kitchen. Oliver grabbed a frying pan while Gavin pulled some bacon and eggs from the refrigerator. After so many years of living together, they worked together quietly and efficiently, whipping up a big breakfast.

"So, I've been thinking…" Gavin started, his gaze looking everywhere but at him.

They never had a problem looking each other in the eye, which meant Oliver knew whatever his foster brother said next was going to piss him off. "Oh yeah?"

"I'm not sure this living situation is working out. Thought it might be a good idea if I head back home, stay with Sean, Chad, and Lauren until the pub and apartment are rebuilt. Give you and Erin a chance to shack up together properly. Good practice for your future marriage."

"No."

Gavin frowned, confused by his short, one-word response. "What?"

"You're not leaving."

Gavin's confusion quickly turned to annoyance. "Don't remember asking for permission, your highness."

"Doesn't matter. I'm not about to let you revert to type."

"What the hell does that mean?"

"Things get tough, someone gets too close, you look for the

closest escape. Took years before you stopped trying to run from me. Now you're doing the same to Erin."

Gavin wanted to argue the point—Oliver could see it in the way his best friend's jaw clenched, but he didn't. That was when he knew his foster brother couldn't argue—because Oliver was right.

"How many people have you let in, Gavin? In your entire life, who do you feel safe enough to truly be yourself with?"

Gavin looked away, and it was obvious he didn't want to answer.

"Me," Oliver said, giving him the easy answer first.

Gavin nodded, still refusing to look in his direction, looking instead out the window. "You."

"And our folks...to some extent. Though I think you still hold back with them too. Never calling them mom or dad, still using their real names, refusing to let them see your scars."

Gavin shrugged but didn't deny Oliver's assertions.

"Maybe Paddy," Oliver said after a minute more. "Not completely, but you've cracked the door, right?"

Gavin nodded, finally facing Oliver again. "A little. Yeah."

"Who else?" Oliver asked, perfectly aware that there was just one more name on the list, and it was a big one.

Gavin picked up a slice of toast, tearing the crust off of it.

"Say it," Oliver prodded.

When Gavin continued to stare at him in silence, shredding his toast to crumbs, Oliver decided it was time to put all his cards on the table. "Erin told me you showed her your scars last night."

Gavin nodded. "Yeah. I did."

"Why?"

Gavin closed his eyes, and that was when Oliver noticed the dark circles under them. Even though he'd just woken up, Gavin was the poster child for exhaustion. Obviously, he hadn't slept any better than Oliver.

"What do you mean, why?" Gavin asked.

Oliver held his gaze. "You've never shown anyone but me. You always wear a shirt with your lovers, and you haven't even let our parents see them. Why her?"

Gavin blew out a long breath. "I don't know why."

Oliver made a buzzer sound. "Errrrr. Nope. Not accepting the cop-out answer. If you really don't know why, then sit there a minute and think about it."

"You're a pain in the ass." Gavin's words were deadpan, completely lacking any emotion.

Oliver laughed. "I'm the product of not one but two psychologist parents. You know as well as I do, we were raised on introspection and self-analysis. Mom and Dad never let either of us get away with nonresponses."

Gavin chuckled. "Jesus. You're not kidding."

"And you do know why you showed Erin, so just say it," Oliver said, putting their conversation back on track.

"I showed her because I wanted her to know..." Gavin paused, considering each word. "To know me better. She thought my mom was dead."

Oliver nodded. "I know. You never corrected that."

"Neither did you," Gavin pointed out.

"Wasn't my story to share. Isn't that sort of the point of trust? Respecting the other person's privacy?"

Gavin took a bite of bacon. "It is."

"Why do you want Erin to know you better? The two of you are already good friends."

Gavin fell silent. Oliver could tell by the look on his face he wasn't going to answer. So he let him off the hook. Again. It was either that, or the two of them would sit in silence for hours on end and they'd never accomplish a damn thing.

"I saw you last night."

Gavin glanced up, frowning. "Last night?"

"I know you watched me and Erin."

He had to hand it to Gavin. The guy's poker face was rock

solid. He cleared his throat uncomfortably. "I should have walked away."

"Why didn't you?" Oliver asked.

Once again, Gavin clammed up.

"Gavin," he pressed.

"Leave it alone, Ollie."

"No. I'm not backing down. Not letting you walk away from this. From us."

"Us?" Gavin scoffed. "There is no us. Just you and Erin, with me hiding in the hallway, skulking in the shadows."

"Why were you hiding?" Oliver prodded, tired of always backing down, always giving Gavin a bye. He wanted answers. He fucking needed them.

"Goddammit." Gavin raked his hand through his dark brown hair, messing the thick mass up. "Just stop already."

Oliver shook his head, even as Gavin's face grew red with anger.

"No. Tell me why you watched us."

Gavin tossed his fork down and it clanged loudly on the plate. Neither of them had eaten more than a few bites. "I couldn't leave!" Gavin shouted, rising and stomping over to the counter, his back turned to Oliver.

"Why not?"

"Because of *her*. Fuck!" Gavin ran his hand through his hair.

"Her?"

"I couldn't stop looking at her. I...I wanted *her*."

Oliver opened his mouth, then closed it, words defeating him.

The silence lingered, but he'd be damned if he could think of a thing to say to that shocking revelation.

"Oh sure. *Now* you shut the fuck up." While his words were light, Gavin didn't turn to look at him. Oliver suspected he was probably afraid of what he'd see.

"Turn around, Gavin."

Gavin lowered his head, shaking it miserably, so Oliver stood up and walked over to him. He leaned his ass against the counter Gavin was staring at intently, determined to avoid Oliver's gaze.

Oliver shifted closer, nudging Gavin with his shoulder. "You want her," he said, not bothering to hide his grin.

Gavin saw his too-pleased expression and cursed. "Please don't."

"Don't what?"

Gavin gave him an exasperated look. "Go where you're going. It was one...weird...night. And...Jesus, I can't believe I'm going to say this, but..." Gavin's eyes traveled skyward as if what he was going to say next would hurt. "I was pretty shaken up after showing her my back. I'm worried my feelings are sort of fucked up. Like...maybe it wasn't attraction. It could have been gratitude or...something...and I've misread it all. Transference or some such shit."

Oliver gripped Gavin's shoulder. "Mom would be so proud of you. That's next-level psychobabble there. I mean...it's completely wrong, but you used a really cool, big word."

"That's super helpful, Ollie. Probably a good thing you followed in Sean's footsteps."

"You want my analysis?" Oliver asked.

Gavin shook his head and crossed his arms. "No. Absolutely not."

Oliver laughed, then forged on. "What I think you're saying is...you actually *are* bi."

His joke hit its mark. Sort of.

While he didn't laugh, Gavin's eyes narrowed, though there was no heat in the look. "You're a fucking asshole."

"I'm a fucking happy asshole."

Gavin sighed. "You know I've never been with a woman. I don't have a clue how...or if..."

Oliver squeezed Gavin's shoulder. "I'll teach you. Now come on. We need to make a list and hit the store. You and I are going to seduce our girl tonight."

Gavin huffed out a harsh breath. "Wow. That escalated quickly. You just totally went there. *After* I told you not to."

"It's me. And I've been waiting for this moment for *fucking* ever. Of course I went there."

"Seriously, Ollie. How about we see how tonight goes before you start picking out china patterns? Maybe we can just have some dinner and talk and...I mean...what if I'm wrong? What if I can't..."

"You can."

"You know, just saying that doesn't make it true. If I can't... Jesus. I don't want to think about what I might screw up if what I'm feeling is wrong. I don't want to hurt her."

"You won't hurt her—you love her—and it's not wrong. We can take it slowly, but we're not walking away from this. Please. Try it. For me. For Erin."

"Erin," Gavin murmured. "What if she doesn't want this?"

Oliver rolled his eyes. "You're joking, right? You were there. You heard her call out your name."

"Why did she do that?"

"Because she wants you, you idiot. She knew you were watching us last night too."

That didn't comfort Gavin, who cursed again. "Shit!"

"It turned her on."

"It did?" Gavin asked.

Oliver nodded. "We both want you to be with us, Gavin. I know it's going to take time for you to believe that, but it's still the truth. And if you open yourself up to what I'm suggesting, if you really give it a shot, then we'll have the rest of our lives to show you how much we love you. How much we need you to be with us."

Gavin glanced away, but Oliver could tell it wasn't a dismissal, rather a way for his foster brother to hide the emotions riding close to the surface. "I've been with you, with your family, for nearly a decade. I wish... I'm sorry I'm not better at..." Gavin ran his hand through his hair again, making his bedhead hairstyle even messier. "For fifteen years, my mother alternated between telling me I was a piece of shit who didn't deserve to be happy to telling me she couldn't survive without me. Makes it hard to hear one thing without waiting for someone to pull the rug out and flip the other way."

"I get that."

"I'm not using that as an excuse, I'm just saying...even now, after all these years with you and Sean and Lauren and Chad, it's hard for me to really believe..."

Oliver pulled Gavin into his arms. "I love you, Gavin. And I'll say it every day, bro. Every day until you believe it."

Gavin hugged him back, and for the first time in his life, Oliver felt like all the pieces were clicking into place.

"So about tonight," Oliver said as they parted. "I think we start with a candlelight dinner."

❧ 8 ❧

Erin walked into the apartment, trying to shake off her exhaustion. It had been a busy shift in the E.R., and all she could think about was stripping off her scrubs, pouring a glass of wine, and conking out on the couch.

That plan changed the second she crossed the threshold and saw Oliver lighting candles on her small dining room table.

He frowned when he saw her. "You're tired."

She nodded. "Yeah. Long day. What's this?" she asked, gesturing to the table.

"You've had quite a few long days lately."

"Short-staffed. Lot of nurses out with the flu. Plus, it's the holidays. Too many suicide attempts and drug overdoses."

Gavin walked out of the kitchen with a glass of red wine in his hand. He handed it to her. "You're late."

"I know. I was just telling Ollie we were slammed. I got stuck filling out some last-minute paperwork. Did we have plans?" she asked.

Oliver shook his head. "Nope."

She considered that for a second, and then panicked. "Are we celebrating something? Oh my God. Did I forget a birthday or anniversary or something?"

Oliver chuckled and repeated himself. "Nope."

She took a sip of wine, glancing from Oliver to Gavin. "Gonna give me a clue here?"

"Gavin and I wanted to do something nice for you. Our way of thanking you for taking us in. Two homeless waifs, out on the street at Christmas."

Erin laughed. "You could have moved back in with your parents."

Gavin shook his head and feigned a shudder. "Two grown-ass men living at home? No thanks. Talk about ruining our street cred."

Erin playfully patted his cheek. "Oh, aren't you cute? You think you've got street cred."

Gavin grabbed her wrist before she could lower her hand. She wasn't sure how to react when he kissed her palm, stroking it just once with a quick brush of his tongue. The kiss distracted her enough that it was easy for him to grab her wineglass and take a big drink.

"Hey," she protested. "That's mine. I really need wine tonight." Before she could reclaim the glass, Oliver reached out and took it, stealing his own sip. Setting the now-empty glass down on the table, he pulled her toward him.

"We'll get you more. We're going to take very good care of you tonight," he said.

"I like the sound of that," she said, not even bothering to shield the weariness in her tone. She really was wiped out.

"Thanks for letting us live here with you, Erin." Oliver sealed his appreciation with one hell of a kiss. The two of them had kissed in front of Gavin plenty of times before, but those had been quick pecks of hello or goodbye. They reserved these kisses —these open-mouthed, lots of tongue, spine-tingling, toe-curling kisses—for when they were alone.

Twice, she tried to pull back, cognizant of Gavin watching and not wanting to make him uncomfortable, but Oliver merely tightened his grip. When he did finally release her, the cocky man had the audacity to give her a wink.

Although, she had to give him credit. She wasn't nearly as tired as she'd been mere seconds ago. He always knew how to help her find her second wind.

"Where's my kiss?" Gavin asked.

Erin gasped softly, uncertain what exactly had happened today between Oliver and Gavin, but clearly she'd missed a step or twenty while she was at work.

"I've never seen the two of you kiss," she whispered.

But holy shit, did she want to.

Gavin shook his head, stepping closer—not to Oliver but to *her*. "I'm not kissing Oliver tonight. We're thanking you, taking care of you, remember? Tonight is all about you."

"But," she started stupidly, "you don't—"

Gavin wiped away any chance she had at finishing that thought. He placed his large calloused hands on her cheeks and drew her to him.

His kiss, like Oliver's, left nothing to the imagination. She was motionless for a full twenty seconds before her brain engaged and told her body to get in the game. Lifting her arms to his shoulders, she parted her lips for him, tasting the wine they'd just shared, on his tongue.

The kiss was surprisingly gentle, despite the intensity of it. Gavin held back nothing, his fingers stroking her cheeks, as if she was made of delicate glass.

She started briefly when Oliver moved behind her, his hands resting on her waist, his chest pressing against her back.

Gavin broke off the kiss, his gaze locked with hers.

Erin held her breath, waiting, hoping, praying. She got a sense Oliver was doing the same, and that he'd positioned himself so that, like her, he would be able to see Gavin's reaction to the kiss. They'd become good enough friends over the past year that she knew she was the first woman he'd ever kissed.

But *why* had he kissed her? What could that mean?

"Put me out of my misery," she whispered when the silence lasted a second or two too long.

"You're the most beautiful woman I've ever met," Gavin said.

Erin drank in the words even as she tried to wrap her head around what was happening.

"What's going on?" she asked, trying to catch up.

"What's going on is we're about to embark on my wild dreams," Oliver murmured, placing soft kisses against the side of her neck.

Erin watched Gavin's face as Oliver explained. He appeared hopeful, yet...reticent?

"Gavin?"

His eyes softened as he cupped her cheek with one hand. "I've never been with a woman, Erin."

"I know," she whispered.

"But I want *you*."

Only Gavin could make a statement like that sound equal parts amazed and anxious. Regardless, she smiled, and even laughed a little. She couldn't help it. It was as if she was feeling happiness for the first time in her life. "Me? Really?" she asked, excitedly, struggling to believe this was all true.

Gavin shook his head, his huge grin matching hers. "God. You and Ollie and these goofy fucking grins. *Yes*, really."

From behind her, Oliver chuckled. "Come on. Let's eat dinner. Something tells me we're going to need the extra calories tonight."

Erin reluctantly stepped out from between the two of them and led the way to the kitchen. "Wow," she said, as Gavin pulled a pot roast from the oven. "That smells incredible."

"It's Aunt Riley's recipe. Called today to get it from her," Oliver said, picking up a knife and slicing the meat. It was so tender, it basically fell apart, and Erin's mouth started to water.

"We were slammed today so I missed lunch. Only managed to choke down a granola bar," she said.

Gavin wrapped an arm around her waist and pulled her close, placing a quick kiss on top of her head. "You work too hard."

She melted inside, loving this new closeness with Gavin. He'd become one of her best friends over the course of the past year despite the rocky start. She'd had to fight hard to push away her attraction to him, comforting herself with the knowledge it wasn't *her* he didn't want but women in general.

"I could say the same thing to you two." Oliver and Gavin had always pulled long hours, never clocking out after an eight-hour day, but those hours had grown even longer since the fire at the pub. She suspected if it was up to them, they'd both work round the clock, desperate to put the pub back together.

Her cousins were making the trip from Philadelphia to Baltimore on Monday to confer with the Collinses about the renovations. If anyone could restore Pat's Pub to its former glory, making it not only look the same but even better, it was the Moretti brothers. She'd spent years watching Tony, Joey, Luca, and Gio work their magic, and she'd said so to Oliver countless times since the fire. She wasn't sure it helped much, though. Too many times over the past week, she'd catch a glimpse of his face —unguarded—and the sorrow she saw there cut her like a knife.

Oliver dipped out three plates while Gavin refilled her wine-glass, plus two more. They all carried their wine and plates to the table. Conversation between the three of them was never an issue, though typically she was the one doing the majority of the talking.

Tonight, that role fell to Oliver, who kept them entertained, retelling silly stories from past holidays with his cousins. She forced herself to listen but found her thoughts constantly drifting as she considered the night to come.

Erin glanced down after several minutes, shocked to discover her plate empty. She couldn't recall what the meal had even tasted like, too distracted. She wasn't sure if it was anticipation or nervousness—probably both—that had her palms sweating, her heart racing a bit too fast.

Oliver's long sigh captured her attention. "We should have skipped dinner. It's obvious the two of you didn't enjoy my efforts."

"Sorry," Erin said sheepishly, aware she should probably feel guiltier than she did. In truth, she was glad the meal was over, excited to move on to the next part.

"Me too," Gavin called over his shoulder. He must have felt the same because he was halfway to the kitchen with his empty plate before she'd even risen.

Oliver chuckled, then reached for her hand, pulling her up. "You're happy, right?" he murmured.

"So happy," she whispered.

He leaned close and gave her a quick kiss on the cheek. "Me too," he said, repeating what Gavin just said.

They followed Gavin to the kitchen, each of them just putting their dishes in the sink.

"We'll clean up later," Oliver said.

The three of them walked down the hall, no one speaking. It should have felt strange, awkward even, but Erin had never felt more certain, more comfortable. While Oliver had told her of his desire for a relationship like the one his parents had, he'd convinced her that dream had changed once he met her. And he'd never—not once—made her feel like she wasn't enough. They'd had more than a few heart to hearts about his childhood and how it had felt to be surrounded by the love of not two but three parents.

Every time they had that conversation, it always ended the same way. With Oliver telling her how much he loved her, how he wanted to spend the rest of his life with her, and how she would always be enough for him.

And she'd never doubted the truth of those words because she had felt the same way.

She knew now they'd both been lying to themselves and to each other. There had been a piece missing.

As they entered her bedroom, Gavin turned and reached out

for her. Drawing her close, he kissed her deeply, passionately, and she suddenly realized he'd been holding back earlier.

When they parted, she glanced over her shoulder and saw Oliver leaning against the doorframe—watching them but apart.

He shook his head at her curious look. "Not tonight."

Before she could question him about that, Gavin cupped her cheek and turned her face back to him, resuming the kiss. It was clear Gavin and Oliver had talked about this, about how things would go. And she was more than happy to follow their lead.

"Take off her shirt," Oliver murmured from the door.

Gavin broke their kiss, never taking his eyes off her, as he reached for the hem of her top—she was still in her scrubs—and pulled it over her head. She recalled doing the exact same thing last night, standing before him in just her bra, so that she could wash out the stain.

However, unlike last night, Gavin didn't look away, didn't try to avoid looking at her body. Tonight, he drank it all in. His gaze felt like a caress as his eyes drifted lower, taking in every part of her.

"Touch her," Oliver whispered.

Erin had been a fool to think Oliver wasn't a part of this. He might not be touching her, but every word he said fueled her arousal, turned her on more.

Gavin ran the tip of one finger along the lace at the top of her bra, gently stroking the curve of one breast, traveling to the valley between, then starting the journey back over her other breast.

Erin took several shallow breaths, suddenly struggling to draw air into her lungs. It was a simple, almost innocent caress, but it packed a punch.

Gavin lifted his hand to her shoulder, slowly drawing her bra strap down, before repeating the same process on the other arm. Using both hands, he drew the lace lower until her breasts were completely revealed.

"Stroke her nipples," Oliver said. "Run your fingers over them. Feel how tight they are."

Gavin responded to everything Oliver told him to do, allowing him to guide them through this experience. Oliver was an intense lover, his dominance in the bedroom completely opposite from his easygoing attitude everywhere else. She, like Gavin, trusted him to know exactly how this should play out.

Erin gasped slightly when Gavin touched her nipples, first with the back of his fingers, then again with his fingertips.

"So tight," he whispered. Erin wasn't sure if he was talking to her or Oliver or, God, maybe himself.

"Pinch them," Oliver said, his voice suddenly husky. He was still in the doorway, too far away, but it was obvious he was feeling the heat, the sexual tension in the room thick as a heavy fog.

Gavin's gaze left her for a moment, traveling over her shoulder to Oliver.

Oliver chuckled softly. "She likes a rough touch. Trust me."

Gavin resumed stroking her and then, he did exactly as Oliver suggested, pinching both of her nipples firmly.

Erin's hands flew up and she gripped Gavin's forearms, not to pull him away but for support. "God," she said, her eyes drifting closed. "Gavin."

He pinched them again, tugging on them as well. "Open your eyes, Erin. I want to see."

She blinked several times, trying to focus. "See?"

"See what this does to you. How it makes you feel. I need to know you like it."

Erin smiled. "I love it. Do you..."

Suddenly, she understood Gavin's need for reassurance.

This was uncharted territory. For both of them. He'd never been with a woman. And she'd never slept with...well...basically a virgin, at least a heterosexual one. Part of her was terrified he'd figure out he'd been wrong about his desires and call it to a halt.

Gavin cupped her breasts, squeezing them tightly. Then he

lowered his head and kissed her again. "You're beautiful. Jesus. I'm blown away by you."

She giggled softly, too happy to keep the sound inside.

"Less talk, more action," Oliver said from the doorway.

Erin glanced over her shoulder, narrowing her eyes. "Come closer."

Oliver sucked in a deep breath, but then did as she said. While he was only a few feet away from them, he still didn't seek to join in. "Reach around her and unfasten her bra."

Erin started to turn around, thinking it might make things easier, but Gavin halted her with firm hands on her shoulders. "Don't move."

He reached around her to unhook her bra. With his arms wrapped around her, it felt almost like an embrace, and she couldn't stop herself from shifting closer, resting her cheek against his strong chest. She longed to see him as well, to strip him of his clothing, but after last night's revelations, she thought it best that he take the lead on undressing himself.

He unfastened her bra with surprising skill, managing the task so quickly and efficiently, she lifted her head and gave him a curious look as he pulled the lace away completely and dropped it to the floor.

"Beginner's luck," he murmured, as she and Oliver laughed lightly.

Erin's laughter ended on a gasp when he resumed his ministrations on her breasts, wasting no time teasing her tight nipples with more pinches, more pulling. He wasn't holding back a thing, and Erin loved it.

"Suck on them," Oliver said at last. Erin had been mere seconds away from making that same demand.

Gavin bent his head, wrapping his lips around one of her nipples. Again, he didn't use kid gloves, but instead took her with a passion that was dizzying. He sucked her nipple hard enough she saw stars. When he grunted, she realized she was gripping his hair, pulling it. She loosened her hold, but Gavin shook his head.

"Pull it harder," he said, just before taking her other nipple into his mouth.

"Gavin likes it rough too," Oliver said.

Erin ran her hands through his hair. She'd foolishly chastised him a few days earlier, telling him he was overdue for a haircut. Now she was grateful he hadn't listened. She loved running her fingers through his thick mass of dark hair, and loved even more the way his groan trembled against her sensitive nipple when she tugged on it, pulled it.

Her back arched with delight.

Gavin lifted his head, his eyes soft with wonder. "Can you come from this?" he asked curiously.

She shook her head. "Not just that. Though it turns me on. A lot." She reached for the bottom of his T-shirt but didn't try to remove it. "May I?" she asked.

Gavin nodded, then helped her pull his T-shirt over his head. She leaned forward, losing no time in running her tongue over his nipple, teasing the tiny bit of flesh with her front teeth. Gavin moaned, his hands gripping her head firmly, holding her lips to his chest.

"Fuck, that feels good."

"Now you know how I feel," she whispered against his tattooed skin. There were fewer scars on his chest, but she was closer to them than she'd been last night, and now—like then—her heart ached for the young boy who'd been so brutalized by his own mother.

She wasn't sure what she'd revealed, but it was clearly too much. Gavin tipped her face up with a firm finger under her chin. "Not tonight, Erin. There's no place for her here. I don't want your pity. Not now, not ever."

She nodded, then decided to put them back on track. Moving forward again, she ran the tip of her tongue from one nipple to the next, then bent over, drawing it straight down his chest to his belly button. She started to drop to her knees, ready to move things along to the next part, but Gavin gripped her upper arms and pulled her upright.

"There's nothing I'd like more than to feel your lips wrapped around my dick, sweet girl, but if we go there, this will all be over too soon. I want to see you. All of you."

Sweet girl.

Oliver's term of endearment. Had he told Gavin? Or had Gavin heard Oliver call her that last night?

She glanced over at Oliver, who was showing amazing patience, given the intense look of desire naked in his eyes. "You're *our* sweet girl," Oliver murmured. "You're always going to be that."

"Ours," Gavin repeated, his fingers finding their way to the elastic waist of her scrubs. He pushed them and her panties over her hips. The soft cotton fell and she toed it off, along with her shoes. She glanced down, surprised to find Oliver kneeling next to them. He bid her to lift one foot, then the other, stripping her socks off for her. That was it. The only touch. Then he lifted one of his knees while resting his weight on the other, resembling a man on the verge of proposing.

"Put your foot on my knee, Erin," Oliver directed.

She did as he said, the position opening her fully.

"Get down here," Oliver said, looking at Gavin.

Gavin dropped to his knees in front of her and Erin reached out, placing one hand on each of their shoulders. It was either that or fall down. Her knees were weak, her body in overdrive. There was something completely overwhelming and sexy as hell about two virile, hot men kneeling before her.

"Ollie," she whispered.

He looked up and gave her a wink that was equal parts charming and amused. He felt it too. The same incredible happiness that kept trying to burst out at the seams.

Gavin was oblivious to their interchange, his gaze locked on her pussy. Once more, Erin felt that slight pang of panic, and she bit her lower lip.

"Touch her," Oliver said, though his command was very nonspecific considering his previous ones.

Gavin lifted his hand, drawing his fingers along her slit from ass to clit. Erin gasped, her grip tightening on their shoulders.

"Slippery," Gavin whispered, gazing up at her. "Hot."

She nodded, unable to speak. Not that Gavin gave her the opportunity. His attention returned to her pussy and he touched her again, running his fingers through her aroused juices.

Lifting his fingers, he paused for just a moment before sucking them into his mouth.

"Fuck," Oliver muttered. "Jesus, man."

If Erin could have found the breath, she might have laughed. Apparently Oliver, the self-proclaimed puppet master of this sex scene, hadn't thought of that, suddenly getting swept away as well.

Gavin touched her again, his fingers now wet. He circled the entrance to her body, gathering up more of her arousal. This time, he lifted his fingers to Oliver.

Oliver hesitated for just a moment, and Erin realized that he'd meant to hold true to his assertion that tonight was just going to be her and Gavin.

Apparently Gavin was changing the game plan. "Just one taste."

That was all the invitation Oliver needed as he sucked Gavin's fingers into his mouth.

Erin fought to remain standing. "Holy shit," she whispered.

Gavin grinned as he pulled his fingers out of Oliver's mouth with a soft pop. Wet now from Oliver's mouth, he moved in once more. This time he stroked the circle of her anus. Erin jerked slightly, her response causing Gavin's eyes to narrow.

"Have you fucked her ass?" Gavin asked Oliver, though his eyes never left her face.

"Just with my fingers," Oliver said.

Gavin's gaze shifted to him. "Why?"

"I was waiting for you," Oliver admitted.

Gavin shook his head with a huff of surprised laughter and Erin appreciated that response. So Oliver had lied to her. He'd never given up on his dream of the three of them. That was becoming more and more apparent as the night went on. If she weren't so damn happy, she'd take him to task for hiding what he wanted from her, from them.

"Ollie," she said softly.

Oliver gave her a sheepish grin. "I'm sorry, Erin."

"It's okay," she whispered.

"God. This was meant to be. You both see that now, right?" Oliver asked, his question equal parts hope and fear. Even now, Oliver was still afraid this dream was just that...a dream.

Neither she nor Gavin bothered to demur or pretend.

Instead, they both nodded.

"We see," she said.

"Touch her there again," Oliver said.

Gavin stroked her anus a few times more, but it was clear his interests lie somewhere else. His fingers drifted back to the opening of her body and he swirled around it several times. "How many?" he asked, though Erin wasn't sure if he was asking her or Oliver.

"Start with two," Oliver murmured.

Gavin pressed two of his thick fingers inside, driving them straight to the hilt without a moment's hesitation.

Erin cried out. "Oh my God!"

"Fuck her with your fingers, Gavin. Pretend it's your cock. Show her what it's going to be like when you finally take her."

Gavin was one of the gentlest souls Erin had ever met, patient and calm, the ultimate caregiver, always tender.

That persona faded away in the bedroom. Like Oliver, it was as if her men had split personalities, living their lives one way when out in the real world, and a completely different way behind the closed bedroom door.

He fucked her roughly with those two fingers, driving deep, hard, fast. Erin shifted her hips toward him, meeting him thrust for thrust. She was perilously close to the edge when the motion stopped.

She opened eyes she didn't realize she'd shut and saw Oliver's hand clenched tight around Gavin's wrist, halting his movements.

"You haven't seen the best part," Oliver said, clearing the huskiness from his throat.

Gavin withdrew his fingers. "Show me."

Oliver drew Gavin's hand the slightest bit upwards, even as Erin shook her head.

"No," she whispered. She was too close. One touch there and she would disintegrate. Not that that was a bad thing. Her resistance was based on the fact she wasn't certain she could remain standing. Especially not on just one leg.

"We won't let you fall," Oliver reassured her, even as he pressed Gavin's fingers against her clit. One touch of Gavin's fingers, driven there by Oliver, and Erin felt the electrical shock of it racing, tingling along her spine.

"Fuck," she said through gritted teeth when Oliver pressed Gavin's fingers against her more firmly, moving them against that sensitive bit of flesh rapidly.

"Use your thumb on her clit," Oliver said. "Keep up that motion."

Erin felt like a marionette in a tornado, her body jerked roughly as Gavin stroked her clit with his thumb.

"Drive those fingers back in." Oliver had taken his hand away from Gavin, moving it to grasp her hip, supporting her weight the best he could, given his position on the floor. "Give her three this time."

Gavin pushed three fingers deep, thrusting in only half a dozen times, his thumb still stroking her clit, before Erin splintered into a million tiny pieces. She doubled over, her elbows landing on the shoulders she'd just been gripping. Oliver, true to his word, didn't let her fall, his hands now firm on her waist, even as Gavin's fingers remained buried inside her. He wasn't using the same force, but he was still moving, drawing her climax out even longer.

Wave after wave of her orgasm crashed against the shore, and just when she thought it was nearly over, Oliver took them all up another level.

"Curl your fingers. There's one more secret place."

Gavin curled his fingers inside her at Oliver's urging and found her G-spot. She jerked roughly as a last, excruciatingly beautiful spasm rumbled through her, and the world went black for one blissful moment.

❧ 9 ❧

"Jesus Christ," Gavin muttered, as Erin's inner muscles finally stopped clenching against his fingers. He started to remove them, gritting his teeth as those same muscles fluttered softly and Erin moaned once more.

Oliver had risen at the end, wrapping his arms around Erin, who'd gone completely slack. Meanwhile, Gavin remained there, on his knees on the floor, trying to wrap his head around what he'd just experienced.

"Motherfucker," he murmured, as Oliver helped Erin to the bed. She was conscious but sort of out of it. She fell to the mattress like a sack of potatoes. Gavin watched it all, even though it felt as if he was having some sort of out-of-body experience.

Once Erin was settled, Oliver returned, reaching underneath his upper arm, helping him to stand.

"Incredible, wasn't it?"

Gavin thought that might be the understatement of the century, but he didn't have enough blood pumping through his brain to do much more than curse. "Son of a bitch."

Oliver laughed. "Imagine how good that's going to feel when it's your cock instead of your fingers."

Gavin shook his head, unable to let himself go there. If he did, he'd come in his pants like an untried schoolboy right this second.

Oliver directed him to the bed. Erin lay sideways on it, naked, her lower legs dangling over the edge. Her face was flushed, her beautiful dark hair spread out like a halo around her head. Her eyes were slitted open, her chest rising and falling rapidly, as if she'd just run a marathon.

"Erin," Gavin said, suddenly concerned he'd gone too far. He'd taken Oliver at his word, trusted him when he said she liked it rough. Gavin's sexual experience with his male lovers had always followed that same line—there was nothing he liked more than a good hard fuck.

"Take off your pants, Gavin," she said, her voice hoarse from her earlier cries. "It's my turn." She pushed herself up on her elbows, her expression the epitome of impatience.

Gavin hesitated, still uncertain, until Oliver slapped him on the back. "Get moving, bro, or I'm going to steal your spot."

"You might try," Gavin taunted as he unbuttoned his jeans, then slid the zipper down. Erin pushed up until she was sitting on the edge of the bed. He took two steps, coming to a stop right in front of her. She reached out to grab his cock, licking her lips, her intent clear, but Gavin grasped her wrist.

"Erin, wait."

He knew the second the words left his mouth it was the wrong thing to say. He'd seen the brief glimpses on her face tonight that said she was still afraid he'd come to his senses and realize he was truly gay, not bi.

Hell, he still harbored his own fears about that, though Erin was doing a pretty good job of wiping those doubts away.

"No," he said. "I don't want to stop. I just…" He ran his hand through his hair, trying to find the words. He'd never struggled to tell his previous lovers exactly what he wanted from them sexually. Though he knew that was because in the past, his emotions had never been engaged. Fucking was just that—fucking. It was easier to make demands, and to follow commands, when the sole purpose was finding sexual completion.

Sex was simple when the only thing either partner cared about was getting off.

Tonight...with Erin...it all mattered too much.

"Say what you want," Erin said.

Gavin glanced at Oliver, who'd removed himself from the picture again. When they'd discussed how they hoped tonight would play out, Oliver had insisted that, for this first time, it should be just Gavin and Erin. His foster brother had reasoned that he'd already had sex with both of them, and they needed a chance to get to know each other—sexually—without him in the way. That had made sense this afternoon when the conversation had just been a hypothetical.

Now that they were here, it was harder to draw a box around each part and call them separate entities.

"I've had blowjobs before," Gavin said. "I've never..."

Erin ran her hands along his thighs, then glanced over her shoulder at Oliver. "Guide us through the next part."

Oliver nodded. "Crawl into bed, Erin." As she shifted on the mattress, he pulled the covers down for her. Then he shook his head at Gavin, clearly annoyed. "Shit, man. Take those damn jeans off."

"I will if you will," Gavin said.

Oliver wanted to reject the request, but Gavin knew what he wanted, what he needed. If Oliver was serious about it being the three of them from now on, then dammit, there was going to be three of them in this bed tonight.

"Ollie," Erin whispered. "Hurry."

Gavin shrugged his jeans off, placing one knee on the mattress, making it clear the next move was Oliver's.

Oliver pulled his shirt and lounge pants off, his cock thick and hard.

Yeah. Just as Gavin figured. Oliver would have suffered in silence the entire time.

"Get in the bed," Gavin said.

Oliver grimaced. "You're not changing the game plan," he insisted. "At least not all of it."

"Is this game plan starting tonight, or should I just go on without you two?" Erin asked, drawing her fingers over her bare stomach and then lower.

Gavin grasped her hand just before she reached her clit. "Bad girl."

"Oooo," Erin said. "I like that."

Oliver sighed. "You tapped into that little kink of hers quick."

Gavin glanced up at Oliver and grinned. "She likes to be punished?"

"Flip her over, spank her ass. Find out just how much."

"Goddammit," Gavin murmured, even as he did exactly as Oliver said. Erin didn't even bother with the slightest token of resistance. Instead, she did most of the work, twisting over, coming up on her hands and knees. Little minx even wiggled her bare ass impatiently.

Gavin ran his hand over her smooth, silky-soft skin, loving the way his touch caused her to shiver. "This wasn't part of the plan," he said, even as he lifted his hand and brought it down firmly.

Erin's skin turned pink instantly, the color, along with her moans of pleasure, all the invitation he needed to continue. He spanked her a few more times, then lifted his chin at Oliver, urging him to get in on the action.

Oliver climbed onto the bed, claiming the other side of Erin. "Spank her again," he said.

Gavin started to insist that Oliver take over, wanting to watch as much as do, but Oliver had other plans.

Oliver drew his fingers along her slit, the touch enough to zap the strength in Erin's arms. Her upper body collapsed to the mattress while her ass remained high, ready.

Before Gavin could read his intent, Oliver pressed two fingers inside Erin's pussy. "Fuck, she's wet."

Oliver's fingers were lodged deep, all the way in, but he didn't move them. Instead, he raised one eyebrow at Gavin, his expression pure "get the fuck on with it."

Gavin lifted his hand again and resumed his spanking. As he peppered her ass with swats, some hard, some light, Oliver fucked her with his fingers.

Erin met them blow for blow, her hands flat on the headboard, the hold adding strength to her backward shoves.

She came within minutes, her body jerking roughly as her legs gave out the same way her arms had. She cried out loudly, gyrating in the most sensuous dance Gavin had ever seen. Men didn't fucking move like that when they came. If anything, they stilled, turned to stone. He preferred her way.

He ran his fingertips along her spine, loving the way she gave herself to the experience completely.

Neither he nor Oliver moved as she lay facedown on the bed between them. He wasn't sure how long they looked at her prostrate form, their own personal nude goddess.

Erin broke the silence, slowly shifting to her back. Her eyes were soft, almost dreamy, when she lifted her arms to Gavin. "I want you inside me."

Oliver lay down next to her, his elbow bent, his head supported on his hand. He reached out to her, cupping one of her breasts.

Once he was in position, he wiggled his eyebrows at Gavin.

"Comfortable?" Gavin said, his voice deadpan.

Oliver chuckled, but Erin didn't reply.

Again that fear, that uncertainty, crept into her eyes. Gavin hated seeing it there. He was determined to drive it away, once and for all.

He glanced to the side of the bed. Erin had two nightstands. For all their planning, he and Oliver had forgotten one pretty important part. "Condoms?" he asked Oliver.

Oliver twisted and opened the drawer of the nightstand closest to him. "Oops."

Gavin started to take it from him, but Oliver shook his head. "Nope. If you get to change the plan, so do I."

Gavin went light-headed as Oliver tore the wrapper open with his teeth before pulling the condom out.

Oliver sat up, grasping Gavin's dick.

"Fuck," Gavin murmured, closing his eyes as Oliver slid the condom in place. "Have mercy, Ollie."

Ollie chuckled, kissing Gavin on the jaw quickly before resuming his spot on the bed next to Erin.

She was slowly coming back to life after her second orgasm. "I've just glimpsed our future," she said softly. "And it's fucking hot."

Oliver cupped her breast once more, but this time he lowered his head, sucking her nipple into his mouth before murmuring, "Yeah, it is. Need directions, bro, or do you think you can take it from here?"

Gavin narrowed his eyes, exchanging a glance with Erin. "Next time, it's his ass we're spanking."

"Deal," she said with a giggle.

Gavin moved as Erin parted her legs, making room for him between. Oliver released her nipple with a pop, scooting over a bit to give Gavin plenty of space.

He gripped his dick in his hand, guiding it to the opening to her body. They shared one more look, both of them smiling almost shyly, before he slid inside.

Gavin took his time, savoring every silky inch as he claimed it. "God, Erin," he whispered. Her name felt like a prayer.

She cupped his cheek, pulling him lower, drawing him into a kiss. He pressed her lips open with his, his tongue finding hers, even as he continued his journey to heaven.

Fully seated, he lifted his head, struggling to believe he was really here. That this was happening.

He'd actually been worried that this wasn't really attraction.

He'd been a fool.

"Erin," he said again, her name somehow freeing him. He lifted his hips, withdrew almost all the way, then powered back in. Erin lifted her legs, locking her ankles around his waist. He felt her fingers on his back, knew she was feeling his scars. In the past, that idea would have repulsed him, but now...he wanted her hands on him. Everywhere.

He moved faster, taking her hard. Part of him wondered—worried—if it was too much. He paused for just a fragment of a second, but Oliver's hand landed on his shoulder.

"Don't stop, Gavin. She's almost there."

Gavin didn't realize he'd closed his eyes, but they flew open when he felt Oliver's knuckles brush against his stomach. Looking down, he watched as Oliver found her clit, stroking it.

Erin's back arched as yet another orgasm rushed through her. Her inner muscles clenched tightly, dragging him down with her.

"Fuck," he shouted. "Holy. Fuck!" The words were ripped out of his chest as jet after jet of come erupted, filling the condom. He briefly wondered what it would be like not to use one. He'd never fucked without a condom, but with her...

God. He was never going to get enough of her.

He felt Oliver's soft kiss on his cheek. He turned, wanting more. Oliver's lips met his, the two of them kissing roughly, hungrily.

"So perfect," Erin whispered, her words drawing their attention.

"Perfect," Oliver repeated.

Perfect, Gavin thought as he withdrew from her, pulled off the condom, dropping it to the floor before he fell to his back, utterly replete and physically exhausted in the best possible way.

Fucking perfect.

＊ IO ＊

Oliver swallowed heavily as he looked around the pub.
The place had been completely gutted, all the soot,
debris, charred wood, destroyed furniture, and shattered glass cleared out. Fortunately, Caitlyn's husband, Lucas,
had a good relationship with the building inspector, who'd come
to check out the building two days after the fire. Once he'd given
them the all clear, assuring them the building was safe to enter,
they'd gone to work on the cleanup quickly, aware that time
wasn't their friend when it came to the threat of mold and
mildew.

All that remained now was an empty shell, no walls, no ceiling, nothing to reveal what this place was or had been.

In his mind's eye, he let himself imagine the pub as it was just
a month earlier, one night while he'd been doing a happy hour
with Erin and Gavin. The place had been crowded with patrons,
watching hockey on the big screen with enthusiasm—alternating
between cursing and cheering. He, Erin, and Gavin had been
drinking pitchers of Guinness, laughing, talking. Pop Pop had
been in the middle of all the action, as always, holding court in
the center of the bar, while Emmy's fingers flew over the
keyboard of her laptop from her spot at the end of the long

mahogany counter, a half-full glass of white wine beside her. Padraig had been pouring drinks, telling tales, entertaining everyone with jokes and sports trivia.

Every inch of wall space had been adorned with sports pennants, antique tin signs advertising different beers, autographed and framed photos of every famous person who'd ever walked into the pub, as well as old black and whites of Pop Pop and Grandma Sunday, back in the early days. It was incredible how many years' worth of memories had been packed into this building, a lifetime of amassed treasures.

And it had all been destroyed, reduced to ash in just one hour.

He jerked slightly when he felt a hand on his shoulder.

"Sorry, son. Didn't mean to scare you."

Oliver turned and smiled at his dad, Sean. He hadn't even heard him come in. "Guess we're the first ones here."

"What about Gavin? Thought he was coming."

Oliver shrugged. "He was at a different work site this morning, but he was planning to be here. Maybe he got held up."

Dad jerked his head toward the entrance. "I just saw the Morettis pull into the parking lot across the street. You okay? You seemed pretty far away there."

Oliver shrugged. "Still struggling to..."

Dad gave him a sad nod. "Yeah. It's hard for me to see it like this too. But you and I both know J and K Construction can rebuild this place, make it even better. All new electrical wiring, plumbing. No more clogged toilets to fight with in the men's room. No more patching that damn crack in the back wall every other year. Better lighting. Whole place has been too long overdue for a fresh coat of paint and the floors in bad need of refinishing. We can do all that now. Make this place shine."

"You're right." Oliver tried to shake off his heavy feelings. His dad always managed to find the bright side in things. And he was confident in his family's skills when it came to the rebuild. Between that and the Moretti brothers' talents when it came to home restorations, Oliver genuinely believed they could return the pub to its former glory. It was just his damn impatience getting the better of him.

They turned to the entrance as Tony Moretti walked in, followed by his brothers, Joe, Luca, and Gio. Bubbles and Aunt Riley had dubbed them the Italian Stallions the first time they'd met the brothers, both of them joking that they'd wasted too many years living in Baltimore if the Morettis were the standard fare in Philadelphia.

Oliver had to admit...Bubbles and Aunt Riley weren't wrong. All four of the Morettis were tall—well over six feet—with broad shoulders, thick muscles, eyes so dark they appeared black, and strong Italian features.

"Down, boy," Dad murmured, obviously noticing Oliver checking them out. Of course, he could have issued the same warning to his dad. They really were birds of a feather, something Oliver's mom and Pop Pop had said at least a million times in the past.

"Sean, Oliver. Good to see you both again," Tony said, walking over, hand outstretched. They all shook hands. Layla's brothers had spent a fair amount of time in the pub over the last couple of years, visiting their sister every two or three months. Oliver figured the reason the Collins and Moretti men had clicked so well was because they all tended to be fairly overprotective of the women in their lives. Though Layla had started joking lately that she didn't think they were coming because they were worried about her anymore, so much as they just wanted an excuse to drink with Miguel and Finn at the pub.

Tony glanced around the building and shook his head sadly, as Joe muttered, "Damn, I just can't believe it. Layla said it was all gone but...still..."

It was their first time seeing the pub since the fire.

"I'm sorry for everything your family lost," Gio said to Sean. "This place was special."

Dad smiled. "Yeah. It was. And with your help, it will be again."

"How's your Pop holding up?" Luca asked.

"He's doing the best of all of us," Oliver said. "Been joking lately that the fire saved him from being the first person in the world to fail at the Marie Kondo method. In Pop Pop's world, everything sparks joy."

Tony chuckled. "That sounds like him."

Dad laughed. "Told Riley she might want to start limiting his TV time. The man is obsessed with home improvement shows these days. I'm sort of surprised he didn't try to crash this meeting. He's got about a million suggestions for the restoration."

"You should have invited him to join us," Tony offered.

Dad considered that, nodding slowly. "Might do that next time. He...hasn't been back here since the fire, so I was hesitant to..."

Tony nodded. "I understand. Next time, we'll meet somewhere else."

"Sounds like a plan. You got the furniture from upstairs, right?" Dad asked.

Luca nodded. "Yeah. Truck brought it all to our warehouse a couple of days ago. I've already started cleaning it up with smoke-damage products. You were smart to get those pieces to us quickly. Gives us a better chance of saving them."

The upper two floors had been mostly saved from burning but had taken a major hit in terms of smoke and water damage. They'd removed the antique pieces Pop Pop had collected over the years with Grandma Sunday that they hoped to restore, renting a moving van for delivery to Philadelphia. Luca was considered one of the best on the East Coast, when it came to refurbishing old furniture, while his twin brother, Gio, was known for his talent for building from scratch—recreating pieces that couldn't be saved.

Dad led them all over to the folding table and chairs they'd set up yesterday for this meeting. On the table was a large stack of photographs, compiled by the entire family, showing different aspects of the pub and restaurant as it had been.

For the next two hours, the six of them sorted through the pictures, discussing what items Tony thought they could find online to purchase—the booths, tables, chairs, vintage glassware, and a lot of the décor fell into that category—and what they would have to build to match, the primary thing being the long mahogany bar. Gio, a master craftsman, assured them he could recreate the bar right down to the scuff marks and scratches if they wanted.

Oliver's phone pinged and he glanced at the screen.

"It's from Gavin," he said, reading the text. "Apparently he was late leaving the last work site. Said there was an incident with his pants and he had to run home. Wants me to tell you guys he's sorry he missed you," Oliver said, glancing up at Tony. He wasn't alone in thinking the Moretti boys were sex-on-a-stick hot. Gavin was going to be pissed he didn't get to check out the eye candy.

"Tell him we said hello. We'll all christen this place with a few pitchers after it reopens," Tony said.

The heaviness Oliver had been feeling upon first arriving had lifted over the course of the meeting. Between the plans J and K Construction had in place in terms of creating a brand-new, state-of-the-art kitchen for Riley and the guarantees of the Morettis that they could restore the pub, could make it look exactly like it had before the fire, actually had him excited to see the end result.

They were just finishing when Riley showed up.

"There are my boys," she said, walking over to the table to hug Tony, Luca, Joe, and Gio. Since her son, Finn, had started dating Layla, Aunt Riley had claimed the Moretti brothers—whose mother passed away when they were younger—as her own. "So what do you think?" she asked, gesturing at the pictures.

While the family had reassured her countless times that the

fire wasn't her fault, the tightness in Riley's shoulders and the haunted look in her eyes proved she hadn't managed to shake the guilt she felt.

"When we're finished, no one will have a clue there'd ever been a fire," Tony assured her.

"I'd like that. A lot. So," she said, "are you finished here?"

Dad nodded. "Yeah, I think we've covered it all."

"Good," Riley said, "because I'm here to kidnap my Italian Stallions. I've got a huge pot of chili and a pan of homemade cornbread with your names all over it. Thought the least we could do was feed you lunch before sending you back to Philly."

Joe wrapped a friendly arm around Riley's shoulders. "Oh yeah. Not about to say no to that offer. Don't tell my aunt, but your cooking is the best on the East Coast."

"Aunt Berta would have your head if she heard you say that—and cut you off from her lasagna forever," Tony joked.

"That's why I said don't tell her."

They all laughed.

Before they could say their goodbyes, Erin showed up.

"Oh, thank goodness," she said from the doorway. "I was afraid I'd miss you."

Tony walked over and picked up his younger cousin, giving her a big bear hug. "Hey there, squeaker," he said, using his nickname for her. Oliver had asked about it once and been told that when Erin was little and she got overly excited, she made a little squeaking nose, while scrunching up her face and pressing clenched fists against her mouth.

After that, he and Gavin had nagged her relentlessly until she'd demonstrated it for them. Now it had become a running joke, he and Gavin imitating it whenever they got excited about something.

Joe joined Tony and Erin, wrapping his arm around her neck to ruffle her hair as she tried to bat him away.

"Dammit, Joey. You're messing it up. I gotta go back to work," she said, though she was laughing.

"That's what you get for not calling me Joe," he said, the response a standard. Apparently he was Joe to everyone in the world with the exception of his family, who insisted he would always be Joey to them.

Oliver reached over and tugged Erin away from her cousin, wrapping his arms around her from behind. "Stop messing with my girl."

Joe slapped him on the back. "Good man. Like the sound of that. Feel better about Layla and Erin living in Baltimore, knowing the Collins men are around to keep an eye on them."

Erin rolled her eyes. "Sweet Jesus, Joey. Caveman much?"

"Easy there, cuz. If Aunt Berta heard you using the Lord's name in vain, she'd wash your mouth out with soap," Gio warned.

"Feel like I want to meet this Aunt Berta," Riley mused. "Get the feeling we'd be good friends."

Tony feigned a shudder. "Not sure the world is ready for that friendship."

Erin laughed. "I concur. And while I said I left Philly for the job, the main reason was so I could expand my cursing vocabulary without fear of Aunt Berta's bionic hearing."

"Unless, of course, Pop Pop is around," Oliver said with a laugh.

"Language," Erin, Oliver, and Sean all said in unison, mimicking his grandfather.

"Do you all want to come for lunch too?" Riley asked, extending her invitation to Oliver and Erin. "There's plenty."

Erin shook her head. "No, thanks though. I'm only halfway through my shift. Wanted to stop by here to see my crazy cousins on my break. I'm going to grab a sandwich in the cafeteria and eat it at the nurses' station. Between the flu bug and people taking time off for holiday events, we're short-staffed, so I promised I wouldn't be gone long."

"I'm out too. Wanna keep working here," Oliver added. "Gavin said since he was home, he'd throw together a few sandwiches for us to eat. The two of us plan to finish framing in the walls on the restaurant side."

"How about you, Sean?" Riley asked.

Dad nodded and rubbed his stomach. "Never gonna turn down your chili, Riley."

The Morettis packed up the photographs before following Riley and Dad outside to head over to Riley's house.

"So Gavin's on his way here?" Erin asked.

Oliver glanced at his phone and nodded. "Yeah. He'll probably be here in a few minutes. You have time to wait? He'll be pissed if he doesn't get to steal some of the same kisses I'm aiming to grab."

He reached out for her as he spoke, robbing her lips of those kisses. His tongue teased her lower lip until she opened her mouth for him. There was something highly addictive about kissing Erin. Maybe it was the way she always tasted like cinnamon—the woman was obsessed with Altoids—or the little mews she made as she kissed, or maybe it was the way she never held anything back.

"I love you," he murmured. The two of them had spoken those words a thousand times in the past year, the emotion attached to them continuing to grow with each passing day.

"I love you too. I get off at four. Will you and Gavin be home for dinner?" Erin asked.

"Oh hell yeah. We're coming home," Oliver said, gripping her hips and pulling her even closer, letting her feel exactly what her kisses did to him. He'd pay for letting himself get so turned on, considering there was no time to take her—and nowhere to hide in the cavernous, bare pub if he did. They'd sealed off the large front window with a huge piece of clear plexiglass—rather than plywood—wanting to allow in as much natural light as possible so they could see as they worked. That meant everyone passing by on the street could glance in and see what they were doing.

Oliver had been touched over the past week by the number of patrons who'd walked by, tapped on the plexiglass, and given them encouraging smiles and thumbs-up. The support from the community had been overwhelming and wonderful.

"But there's a different hunger I'm hoping the three of us can take care of when we get there," he said, reluctantly releasing her.

Erin refused to break their union, wrapping her arms around his waist more tightly and resting her cheek against his chest. Erin was a huge hugger. "Something tells me after the last two nights, you're going to be insatiable for a while."

Oliver placed a soft kiss on the top of her head. "I haven't had a chance to talk to you alone since..."

"Since Gavin and I..."

Neither of them seemed capable of saying the words. Oliver pulled away slightly, cupping her cheeks in his hands. "It's as perfect as I think, right?"

Erin grinned. "More than perfect," she whispered.

"You're right, it is."

They broke apart, turning toward the folding table where Gavin stood, smiling at them.

"You have a bad habit of spying on us," Erin teased.

Oliver picked up on the joke. "Especially since it's more fun when you actually join in rather than watch."

"I didn't hear you bitching about being in the audience Saturday night," Gavin said, as he crossed the pub toward them. "In fact, seems to me, you liked watching me and Erin. A lot."

Oliver sighed. "You got me there." Originally, he'd intended to remain completely apart from the action for their first time, but in the end, there'd been no way he could be so close to the two loves of his life and *not* kiss them, touch them. "Why are you late?"

Gavin groaned and gave them an amused grimace. "I'd like to ignore that question, but I know there's no way the guys at work aren't going to fill you in, and I'd rather tell the story my way."

Oliver chuckled as he rubbed his hands together. "This should be good. What happened?"

11

Gavin pointed down to his jeans. "Had to go home to change my jeans. I was late leaving the other work site and pissed about it because I wanted to see the Morettis."

"Tony looked hot today. Had his hair down," Oliver said, wiggling his eyebrows.

"Damn," Gavin said as he sighed. Tony Moretti wore his hair long, and it was fucking hot.

Erin rolled her eyes, though she was used to Gavin and Oliver ogling her cousins. "You two are lucky my self-esteem is unshakable, or you'd give me a complex."

Gavin laughed. "Your family has good genes, and you got the best of them, gorgeous."

Oliver ruffled her hair playfully. "Besides, you have to be used to people checking those guys out. Hell, even Dad was giving them a second glance."

Gavin snorted. "Sounds like Sean."

"No more talk about my sexy cousins. I forbid it," Erin said. "Why did you have to change your jeans?"

"Like I said, I was late. And rushing. Caught the damn back

pocket of my brand-new jeans on a nail and ripped one whole ass cheek out of the things."

Erin and Oliver cracked up.

"Oh man, I would have paid money to see that," Oliver said, slapping his foster brother on the shoulder.

"Yeah, well...let's just say I picked a bad day to go commando."

Erin squealed loudly. "Oh my God. No! That's hilarious!"

Gavin was struggling to find the humor in it all. "You know the guys on the crew, Erin. They're not going to let this go."

"Damn right, they're not. You're going to be the butt of jokes for weeks," Oliver said, laughing even harder.

"Asshole," Gavin muttered with no heat, fighting to hide his own grin. "Anyway, I backed my way out of there—" He had to pause as Erin and Oliver lost it again, guffawing over his use of the word "back" in the description of his escape. Once they settled down, he quickly finished the story. "I went home, changed my jeans, made us some lunch—" He gestured to the brown paper bag he'd put on the folding table while watching Oliver and Erin kiss. "And hightailed it over here."

Erin glanced at Oliver. "Are we going to let hightail go?"

Oliver winked at her, his smile huge. "Better pace ourselves."

"Think Lauren can fix the jeans with her sewing machine? They were brand-new jeans. First time I've worn them," Gavin asked Oliver, grateful Lauren had taken up quilting. He'd lived enough of his life poor as shit that he couldn't stand the thought of tossing a pair of jeans he'd only worn a few hours, but God knew he was hopeless with a needle and thread.

"Depends on where the rip is. Seam's easy. If it's the actual material, trickier," Erin said, glancing at her watch. "Damn. I really do need to head back."

Gavin grasped her hand and tugged her close. "Didn't get to steal my own kisses yet." He placed his lips on hers, marveling at how much he enjoyed kissing her.

Her.

Before Erin, he'd never felt the desire to be with a woman. Hell, it had even sort of repulsed him to think about. Now...he was quickly becoming addicted to sleeping with her snuggled between him and Oliver in bed.

Oliver stepped closer as they kissed, the three of them forming a tight circle. "Got room for me in there?" he asked, wrapping one arm around Erin's back, the other around Gavin's.

Erin turned her face to Oliver and began kissing him as Gavin ran his lips over her soft cheek, then Oliver's rougher one.

When they parted, Gavin was there, ready to steal another kiss, this time from Oliver.

"Dammit," Erin murmured as she watched them kiss. "That is seriously hot. And I am seriously late."

He and Oliver chuckled as they broke apart.

"We'll pick up where we've left off tonight," Oliver said.

"Sounds good." Erin reached into her jeans pocket and pulled out her key fob. "Walk me to my car?"

The three of them walked out into the bright sunshine, shifting closer to ward off the chilly December air. Oliver held Erin's hand as Gavin wrapped his arm around her waist. They crossed the street to the parking lot and stepped next to the driver's door of her Volkswagen Jetta.

Erin kissed each of them once more, obviously reluctant to leave, then she lifted the fob over her shoulder and hit the button to unlock the door.

"See you at home tonight," she said, lifting her face for yet another kiss.

Oliver chuckled, then deepened the next kiss, going out of his way to keep her with them. The entire thing reminded Gavin of those first love middle school phone calls, where the couple argued over who should hang up first.

He was just about to enter the game when he heard his name.

"Gavin."

His heart stopped for one beat, two. When it started again, it was racing a million miles an hour.

He turned slowly, deliberately stepping forward as he did so, placing himself directly between Erin and Oliver and...

"Mom."

He was still close enough to his lovers that he felt Oliver jerk behind him, though his attention was solely focused on her.

The nine years since they'd seen each other hadn't been kind to her. She was even thinner than before, something he hadn't thought possible. His mother had always been a frail woman, skin over bones. He'd had plenty of time to consider that as he thought about all the beatings he'd taken from her. By the time he was eleven, he'd been bigger than her and definitely strong enough to stop her.

He hadn't, and he knew—even in the midst of the pain she wrought—it was because he was cognizant of how fragile she was, and he hadn't wanted to hurt her. So he'd turned his back in an attempt to mitigate the damage while seeking ways to escape.

Right now, it looked as if a strong wind could blow her over.

Her hair had always been dark brown, but it was more salt than pepper now, and she'd cut it shorter, the ends barely brushing her bony shoulders. There were more wrinkles around her eyes and mouth, tight lines that proved this was a woman who never smiled, only scowled.

That fact was proven when she fought to smile at him now, the attempt shaky at best.

"Gavin," she said again, her voice thin, reedy.

"How did you find me?" he asked.

"I ran into Ms. Johnson at the grocery store. Remember her? She lived on the third floor of our old apartment building."

Gavin silently cursed in his head. He'd done some work for Ms. Johnson, an elderly woman who had been kind to him when he was younger, always waiting for him at her door when he got off the bus with some treat—cookies or crackers or a slice of homemade bread. To a starving little boy, she'd felt a bit like his own personal fairy godmother, and he'd never forgotten her.

Part of him suspected she'd been the one to call the cops that night his mother had been committed, though she'd never admitted it and he'd never asked.

He'd gone to visit her earlier this year on a whim, driven by the desire to thank her for her kindness to him when he was a kid. While in her apartment, she'd asked if he could take a look at her oven, which had stopped working. He'd fixed it, then given her his number, telling her she could call him if she had any more trouble with it.

Since then, she'd called him once every couple of months, asking for his help with something else that was broken. He'd gone to help her every time, certain her requests were based less on her desire to fix things and more because she was lonely.

She'd never asked about his mother—he figured there were very few tenants in the rundown building who didn't know about her being committed—and he'd never offered any information. Instead, he told her about his job and how he lived above Pat's Pub.

"I remember her," he said, his chest suddenly tight as he wondered how his mother had managed to trick Ms. Johnson into revealing where he lived.

"Look at you," she said, her eyes taking him in from head to foot. "You've grown to be such a handsome, strong man." It looked like she wanted to say more but stopped herself, her gaze traveling to his right, then his left.

Gavin followed the direction of her eyes and realized Oliver and Erin had moved forward and were now flanking him. There was no mistaking their obvious disdain—and perhaps anxiety— as they looked at his mother.

"I..." His mother hesitated. He knew what she was waiting for, but he'd be damned if he'd introduce his mother to Oliver and Erin.

Oliver took the choice away from him. "I'm Oliver Collins."

"Collins," his mother murmured. "You're Sean and Lauren Collins' son?"

"And Chad's," Oliver added.

Gavin didn't miss the slight wince on his mother's face when Oliver mentioned Chad. She'd made her feelings about homosexuals—she called them "queers"—very clear for years. He'd never come out of the closet to her, even though he'd known he was gay from the time he was old enough to understand the concept.

"Ollie, this is my mother, Cecilia Hawke." Gavin swallowed heavily before placing his arm around Erin's shoulders. "And this is Erin Cafferty."

His mother gave Oliver and Erin a nervous smile, probably because neither of them was bothering to hide their true feelings for her. Erin had only seen his scars for the first time a couple nights ago, and as such, her anger toward his mother was still new, still burning hot.

Although, longevity didn't seem to help cool things off. After all, Oliver had seen the scars countless times over the past few years, and his rage was just as apparent, just as powerful.

Gavin turned to Erin. "You're going to be late," he murmured, hoping he could convince her and Oliver to leave. This reunion was going to be difficult. He didn't have a clue what he wanted to say to his mom and trying to figure that out, while also attempting to keep Oliver and Erin calm, was absolutely beyond him at the moment.

"I don't care," she whispered.

"Erin." He hoped the two of them were speaking low enough that the traffic on the street would drown out their words, keep his mother from overhearing them.

"I'm not leaving," she murmured, her voice tight with anger, determination.

"Please," he mouthed.

Erin studied his face long and hard. She knew him well enough to read his expressions, so there was no doubt she could see how desperate he was to do this on his own. Her face softened and her shoulders slumped. "I'm calling you. In one hour. And you're picking up the phone."

"Okay. I promise."

Finally, she nodded, and then without sparing another glance for his mother, she turned and got in her car. He, Oliver, and his mother stepped away from the vehicle as she backed out and left.

One down, one to go...

A quick look in Oliver's direction told Gavin that this one was going to be a hell of a lot harder to convince.

"Ollie," he started, but Oliver shook his head.

"You're not surprised," he murmured, but his mother didn't appear to have heard.

"Didn't your foster parents tell you I was out?" his mother asked Gavin. "I called Lauren. She wouldn't give me your number."

"I know," Gavin said, hating the look of surprise on Oliver's face. He hadn't meant to intentionally hide the fact his mother was out of the hospital, but...he'd had a hard enough time coming to grips with it himself. Plus...

Gavin lifted his hand, gesturing toward the pub. "We've been kind of busy."

It was a lame excuse, and Oliver called him on it. "Not *that* busy."

Gavin opened his mouth, hoping he could convince Oliver to go back to the pub, but Oliver scowled and muttered, "Save your breath."

Oliver wouldn't be moved. And it suddenly occurred to Gavin he was okay with that. Fifteen-year-old Gavin had lived a solitary life, firm in the belief that the only person he could count on was himself. It had taken Oliver the better part of a decade, but he'd shown Gavin the value of having someone at his back, someone to love and support him.

He turned toward his mother again, resisting the urge to end the conversation here. At least until he figured out what the hell he wanted to say to her.

It was clear Erin and Oliver thought he should rant and rave and rail at her for all the pain she'd caused him. He couldn't blame them for that. All they saw were the scars. They didn't have the history to go along with it. They'd only seen and heard the bad, which was Gavin's fault. He hadn't told them about the other times, when his mom was sober and working and, well... trying. Now that he understood her mental illness, it made it even harder to blame her because he knew she couldn't control a lot of what she'd done, at least not without medication, which they wouldn't have been able to afford.

"Ms. Johnson said you live above the pub." His mother looked at the burned-out building.

"We did," Gavin said. "Until a week or so ago. Obviously, that's changed."

"I can see that. Were you home?"

Gavin nodded. It had been radio silence between he and his mother for nine years, so the fact they were standing on the street having a somewhat normal conversation was disconcerting.

"I'm so glad you're okay. Where are you staying now?"

Gavin didn't want to reply to that. "At a friend's place," he responded vaguely.

Her gaze slid to Oliver. "With him?"

"What do you want?" Gavin asked, refusing to share any details of his personal life with her.

"I missed you, Gavin," she said, her voice betraying how close she was to tears. The uncharitable part of him wondered if they were genuine or her attempt at manipulating his emotions.

He silently hoped she managed to control them. Her crying had been his undoing too many times. She'd wake up the morning after losing her temper, take one look at his cuts, burns, and bruises, and fall apart, crying, hugging him, telling him she was sorry, and swearing she'd never hurt him again.

Maybe he should have spent some time on Lauren's psychology couch and asked her what it was about him that made him feel like he had to provide comfort to his abuser in those moments, because that was the part he was struggling with now. He'd hated to see her sad, so he'd forgiven her—time after time—and said he loved her, that it was all okay.

Oliver remained quiet, but Gavin felt him shifting just a tiny bit closer, letting him know subtly that he was there for him.

"Mom—" he started, desperate to cut this reunion short. Seeing her, on the heels of losing everything in the fire, and after this weekend with Erin and Oliver, was simply too much. He was on emotion overload.

She must have heard the dismissal in his voice because she cut him off. "I know I don't have the right to ask...to..."

Oliver scoffed. It was quiet, but it was enough to throw his mother off.

Gavin glanced at his foster brother and shook his head, just once. Oliver frowned, but he remained quiet.

"What do you want?" Gavin asked again, and the pain that question caused felt a bit like he was pulling a stake from his heart.

She visibly swallowed, then cleared her throat. "I was hoping to get to know you again. To spend time with you. And..." She glanced at Oliver. "Maybe your foster brother." He heard the question in her voice. No doubt she'd witnessed he and Oliver both kissing Erin a few minutes ago. "And your girlfriend?"

Now she was outright fishing. But he wasn't going to give her anything. To do so would be opening a door, giving her hope for something he...

He ran his fingers through his hair, frustrated with himself because damn if he wasn't feeling it. That first horrible spark of hope.

Hope that she'd changed.

That this time would be different.

That she'd finally be a true mother.

What the fuck?

Why was all of that still there? He knew better.

Or...he *should* know better.

He felt Oliver's hand on his lower back. He was shocked that a gentle touch could have such a powerful impact. He stiffened his spine.

"I'm not sure that's a good idea." Gavin inwardly groaned. It was a shitty response, one that left way too much wiggle room.

"I understand," she said. This time, the words were completely broken and tears began to slide down her face.

Gavin fought to take a breath, even as he felt the walls closing in on him. Oliver's hand fisted in his shirt, another sign that he was there for him.

"I know I hurt you. I don't know why I grabbed that knife."

The knife? That was what she remembered as the bad part?

Gavin waited for some reaction from Oliver, but his foster brother stayed silent.

"I shouldn't...have come here. I just...wanted...to tell you... how sorry I am. For all of it. You're...all I have, Gavin. All I have in the world." Her words were now coming out in panting breaths, staggered by stuttered sobs.

He closed his eyes, trying to block out her face, her words. How many times had she told him that before? Reminded him, guilted him, made sure he knew he was her whole world. He was it. The kid in him always fell for it, always let those words excuse her rages because he knew they were true. And because it had made him feel like his life had a purpose. Because to one person, he was the center of the universe.

When he opened his eyes, he truly let himself *see* her. Not through the eyes of a kid but as a man.

"You have family," he said. Gavin had been surprised to discover he had a grandmother and an aunt—both living in different states—the first time Margie had come to remove him from his mother's care when he'd been seven years old. He hadn't met either of them because neither had been willing to take him in. At the time, he'd been furious with them, but after too many years at the hands of a sociopath, he could almost understand why they'd want to keep their distance from Cecilia Hawke. He couldn't wrap his head around leaving a defenseless child in her care, but he knew enough to understand that even cracking a door open to his mother left a person at risk.

His mother blinked a few times in surprise. He'd never told her he knew about them.

"Yes, but…I…they threw me out, they wouldn't help me—*us* —they left us alone to survive, Gavin. Never sending money, never offering anything."

"Listen—" he started, but once again, she forged on.

"Please, Gavin. Please! I just want to talk to you. Get to know you again. Maybe dinner? Just one night. That's all, I swear. One night, and I'll leave you alone forever if that's what you want." Then, because she was a master when it came to pushing all the right buttons, she added, "It's the holidays. It's just so hard…this time of year…to be by myself. I've missed so many Christmases with you."

Gavin studied her face as a million different feelings crashed in on him at once. He glanced over at Oliver, certain his foster brother was busting at the seams, ready to read him the riot act for even considering her request.

What he saw on his best friend's face proved Gavin was wrong.

Oliver gave him a sad smile, slowly shrugging one shoulder that clearly said this was Gavin's call, and he'd support him no matter what.

He rubbed his hands together before stuffing them in his pockets, trying to combat how cold he suddenly felt. He wasn't sure the chill was so much because of the weather or if it was brought on by his anxiety…and a fear he hated admitting to feeling.

"Fine. One dinner. But that's all."

His mother smiled as she wiped the tears from her cheeks,

and Gavin instantly regretted what he'd agreed to. He'd just done what her mother and sister had been smart enough to avoid.

He'd opened the door a crack.

When he should have slammed it in her face.

Erin was pacing in the living room, waiting for Oliver and Gavin to get home. Oliver had texted a few minutes earlier to say they were leaving the pub and that they'd be there soon. She had called Gavin this afternoon, just as she'd said she would, but she'd had to cut the call short when several ambulances arrived, carrying victims from a bad car crash.

Gavin had assured her he was fine and that they could talk about it all tonight.

Well, it was tonight. And she was holding him to that.

She glanced up when she heard the key in the door. Oliver crossed the threshold first, followed by Gavin.

He gave her a weak smile when he spotted her. No doubt her anxiety was flashing brighter than a damn strobe light.

"I'm okay, Erin," he said, striving but failing to convince her.

She could understand that. "I think I would have freaked out if I'd thought the mother I hadn't seen in nine years and who was in a psych hospital just showed up, all of a sudden, on my doorstep..." Her words faded away when Gavin and Oliver exchanged a glance, and she realized something she hadn't before. "Wait. You knew she was out. Didn't you? That's why you were so calm." She'd chalked up his quiet, almost nonexistent reaction to his gentle, typically unshakable nature.

Gavin nodded. "Aaron told me a few days before the fire. I was going to tell you both, I swear."

Erin wasn't sure if she felt better or worse knowing that Gavin had kept the secret from Oliver as well. She wondered if Gavin would ever be able to fully open himself up to them. Not that she blamed him for playing his cards close to his chest. She'd seen the scars, and while she hadn't heard the stories, every single one of those puckered or slashed places on his skin told her more than she needed to know. More than she wanted to know.

Like Oliver, she'd grown up in a huge family, loved by her parents and sisters, adored and doted on by her aunts and uncles and grandparents, and never lonely, thanks to countless cousins to play with.

For the majority of Gavin's childhood, it had just been him and...that woman. Even now, Erin was kicking her own ass for walking away this afternoon. It had been on the tip of her tongue to tell Cecilia Hawke off. Countless horrible words had fought their way to the surface, but one look at Gavin's face had kept her silent.

Those words weren't hers to say.

They were his.

Oliver placed a comforting hand on Gavin's shoulder. "It's fine, man. I told you. It's okay."

Gavin and Oliver had spent the entire afternoon together and it was obvious they'd done a lot of talking. She was glad they'd managed to come to some sort of understanding, even though she was sorry she hadn't been there.

Gavin looked at her and she could tell he was worried she would hold a grudge.

"I'm not mad, Gavin. Jesus. On top of the news your mom was out, you lost everything you owned to a fire and had sex with a girl for the first time. I think I can cut you some slack." And then, because she desperately wanted to see him smile, she added, "This time," with a raised eyebrow that told him he wouldn't always get an easy bye.

He gave her something better than a genuine smile. He actually laughed, and the tightness in her chest loosened for the first time since meeting Cecilia.

"I've never told you anything good about her," Gavin said quietly.

Erin wanted to say there wasn't enough good the woman could do to make up for the scars, but she bit her tongue, aware that her anger wouldn't help Gavin. "So tell us something good," she said instead.

Gavin thought for a moment, then said, "We didn't have a lot of money. When she was working, it was usually as a waitress, and she put in long hours, trying to make ends meet with her tip money. She was rarely home when I got out of school, so I spent a lot of time at the park playing basketball, until it was time to go home and make dinner for us. I didn't have my own ball, so I always had to wait for someone to invite me to play with them. On my eleventh birthday, she surprised me with a basketball, even though I knew we couldn't afford it." Gavin smiled. "I loved that ball. Even slept with it."

Oliver grinned. "That's cool."

"Yeah." Gavin's face sobered, and it was clear to Erin they were missing part of the story.

She tilted her head, studying his face.

Gavin ran his hand over his jaw and grimaced. "Probably should have come up with another example."

Oliver's expression darkened. "What did she do to the ball?"

"Woke up one night to her..." Gavin swallowed heavily. "Putting a cigarette out on my back. I jumped out of bed and crossed the room to get away from her. I was getting bigger and faster, so she couldn't hold me down like she had when I was little. My ball was..." He fell silent.

"She popped the ball," Erin said, shaking her head.

Gavin nodded. "Fuck. What I was trying to explain—even though I did a shit job—was my mom wasn't always cruel. There were a lot more days when she was sober and lucid than when she was drunk and..." He lifted one shoulder as if he didn't want to say the word. Finally, he forced it out. "Crazy."

"Cruel," Erin amended.

Gavin didn't respond to her correction. "I'm tired," he said.

"Tired of what?" Oliver asked.

Gavin shrugged. "Just tired. Spent most of my childhood fighting to stay with my mom, trying to get away from the foster homes and back to her because I love—loved—her."

Erin heard the question in his voice when he tried to change the word love to past tense.

"Sometimes I wonder if I'm crazy too," he admitted.

Oliver shook his head. "You're not crazy." He placed his hand on Gavin's back and led him to the couch. The three of them sank down together, she and Oliver flanking Gavin. "Your feelings are yours, Gavin. You can love your mother, you can hate her, you can feel nothing. There's no right or wrong, bro."

"I think that's my problem. I don't know how I feel about her."

"That's okay too." Erin lifted Gavin's arm and dropped it around her shoulders so she could snuggle closer to him, wrapping her arms around his middle. Even though they were sitting hip to hip to hip, Gavin looked like a man adrift alone in the middle of the ocean.

"Actually, I think what I feel the most is guilty."

Oliver frowned. "What the hell about?"

"She looked...sad today. I mean, she's living in a halfway house after being locked away nine years. It's gotta be tough for her, trying to figure out how to start her life again and I'm the only family she has."

Erin lifted her head from Gavin's shoulder. If there was one thing Erin loved most about Gavin, it was his giving nature. She knew all about the elderly lady from his childhood that he'd started doing chores for. Just like she'd watched him fix countless things in pretty much every Collins family member's house. Hell, he'd tackled no less than twenty projects in her apartment over the last year. If he saw someone in need, Gavin didn't hesitate to help.

But she could see now that incredible character trait was working against him.

"Your mom isn't your responsibility," she said, even as she knew the words wouldn't land.

"That's just it. She is. She always has been. I told you. She worked long hours, trying to support us. So I took care of the other things."

"Like?" Oliver prodded.

"I cleaned the apartment, cooked our meals, shopped for food. I even learned how to forge her signature on her checks and took over paying the bills. She's crap with money. When we didn't have enough," he swallowed heavily, "I stole it. I just don't know how she's going to be able to—"

"Stop," Oliver said. "Stop right there." Oliver squeezed Gavin's thigh. "She's an adult and she'll learn. Shit, she should have learned all that stuff before now instead of foisting it off on a kid."

Gavin sighed. "I didn't mind doing it."

"That's not the point," Oliver countered. "Why are you tired, Gavin?"

Gavin closed his eyes wearily. "I don't know."

"Yes, you do," Oliver persisted.

Gavin turned his head toward Oliver, his gaze narrowed. "You gonna make me spew a bunch more bullshit psychobabble."

Oliver chuckled. "I like it when you try to use some of Mom and Dad's big words. It's cute." He placed a quick kiss on Gavin's cheek, and Erin giggled softly.

"Asshole," Gavin muttered, though there was no anger behind the word. Only amusement.

"Gavin," Erin started. "You spent your whole childhood

taking care of your mom, shouldering too many burdens because..." She hesitated when she realized she'd backed herself into a corner.

Gavin let her off the hook, saying the hard words for her. "Because I thought if I took care of her, if I fed her and kept the house clean, took all the stress out of her life, she wouldn't go back to that dark place, she wouldn't drink. She wouldn't...hurt me."

"Do you want her back in your life?" Erin asked.

Gavin lifted one shoulder, then fell silent. She and Oliver waited patiently, giving him time to think it through. Finally, he said, "I don't know. I think that's why I'm so tired. I can't figure this out. I know she's bad for me, but I... Jesus, she's still my mom, you know?"

Oliver reached out and cupped Gavin's cheek. "So stop trying to figure it out. You don't have to come up with an answer tonight or tomorrow or even next week."

Erin smiled, agreeing with that advice, the tension suddenly broken. They'd tackle this as a team. "It's the holidays. Why don't we just focus on that? Relax and enjoy being together. We can think about the rest of it later. We'll help you sort it all out. You don't have to do any of this alone anymore."

"But...I told her I'd..." Gavin blew out a long breath.

"Told her what?" Erin asked.

"She wants to go out to dinner with him," Oliver said. "Gavin agreed."

And just like that, Erin's stress was back and she was ready to put her foot down. "What?"

Gavin was seriously conflicted about his feelings for his mother, and after everything he'd been through, she didn't want him to suffer a single second more if she could prevent it. She hadn't really been joking earlier about her reasons for cutting him slack. The poor guy was on system overload.

"Whenever it happens, we're all going," Oliver hastened to add. "You, me, and Gavin."

Her gaze flew to Gavin's face to see if that was true.

Gavin nodded. "We're all going," he repeated. "I mean, if you—"

"I'm going." She didn't want him to question that for a second. Or try to cut her out.

"Then we've settled everything we need to settle for tonight. So how about a distraction?" Oliver suggested.

The tension in the room lifted when Gavin almost visibly shook off his sadness and gave Oliver a wicked grin. "What did you have in mind?"

"Did you start dinner yet?" Oliver asked her.

Erin shook her head. "I have some chicken marinating. Won't take me a minute to pan fry it. I made a tossed salad too. After all the heavy meals we've had lately, I thought it wouldn't hurt us all to eat something light for a night."

"I agree," Oliver said. "And I'm glad you're not cooking yet. We can eat it after."

Erin rolled her eyes as Gavin rubbed his hands gleefully.

"You both have a one-track mind," Erin chastised, hoping neither of them called her out. Because there was no denying her train was on the same rails and right behind them. Shit, she was probably in front of them.

Oliver raised his eyebrows. "Are you trying to tell me you'd rather eat a light dinner over working up a little appetite before-hand? Because if so, I've terribly misjudged you."

Erin laughed as she stood and started down the hall. She didn't bother to look over her shoulder as she called out, "Last one to the bedroom has to watch me give the other one a blowjob."

She probably should have considered her taunt more care-fully when the thunder of feet came barreling down the hallway behind her, and she recalled exactly how competitive Gavin and Oliver were. She'd only just managed to get in the bedroom when she heard a loud crash against the wall outside her door.

Erin turned and laughed when she saw Oliver and Gavin in

an honest-to-God, true-brothers shoving match, trying to be the first to get into the room.

She raised her hands in a gesture of peace. "Forget it. Blowjobs for both of you."

Just like that, they stopped jostling for position and walked into the bedroom. Their matching looks—primal, hungry, dominant—had her rethinking once again. "Or um…" she said, backing across the room until her legs hit the baseboard of the bed. "Maybe you both should just go down on me."

"Seems to me," Oliver mused to Gavin, "we've been letting our sweet girl think she can call the shots in the bedroom. You getting that feeling, Gavin?"

Gavin crossed his broad arms, the act drawing her attention to just how built he really was. "I am, but I'm the new guy here. Just figured you were too indulgent, letting her get her own way. She's kind of spoiled."

Oliver chuckled, the sound somehow both menacing and hot as hell. "There's no *kind of* to it. She's very spoiled."

Erin fought to school her features, but she was a sucker for a dominant man and when faced with not one but two, well…she was pretty sure she'd been a damn saint in a prior life to deserve this.

She must have failed to hide her excitement because Gavin narrowed his eyes.

"She doesn't appear to be taking this seriously."

Erin winked playfully, hoping to poke both her tigers. It worked.

Gavin reached out, twisting her until her back was pressed against his rock-hard abs. He wrapped his arms around her, banding her waist with one forearm, her breasts with the other. Her entire body went into overdrive when he shifted the arm on her breasts higher, his large hand coming to rest just at the base of her throat.

She didn't even bother to try to break free. Gavin's muscular arms felt like steel chains and she loved it.

Oliver cupped her cheek, the touch almost gentle compared to the dark, penetrating look in his eyes. "You going to behave for us, sweet girl? Or do we need to tie you to that bed?"

Erin bit her lower lip. Oliver had introduced her to bondage a couple months earlier, and it had been some of the most intense, incredible sex of her life. Since then, they hadn't had a chance to revisit it. Primarily because they'd both had roommates up until a couple weeks ago, and even with the gag Oliver had placed between her lips, she'd been way too loud and completely incapable of restraining her cries.

"Oh, I think we both know you're going to have to make me behave," she taunted.

Oliver's smile radiated pure dominance. "Good answer." He turned and walked to her closet. He'd been in her room enough to know her collection of scarves hung on a hook on the back of the door. He helped himself to four of them as Gavin, who still held her, began kissing the side of her neck.

She jerked and cried out when he sank his teeth into the sensitive place where her neck turned into shoulder.

"Gavin," she breathed, hoping to entice him to bite her again. Before he could give her what she wanted, Oliver was back. He lifted his chin up just once, silently indicating something Gavin must have understood.

Gavin released her and she instantly missed his strong arms. She did a quarter turn so she didn't have her back turned to either of her lovers. The game was on and she intended to give them a run for their money.

She grinned as she took a half step back, slowly moving toward the bedroom door. The idea of making them chase her appealed more than she could say.

"I wouldn't suggest it," Gavin said, the rumble in his voice doing wicked things to all the fun parts of her body. Her nipples tightened while her pussy clenched in anticipation.

"Suggest what?" she asked coyly, even as she took another step back.

Oliver shook his head, but he didn't say anything. Instead, he wrapped one of the scarves in his hand around his palm in a way she was certain he'd intended to be menacing. The shame of it was, it ratcheted her arousal even higher.

"Get undressed," Gavin said.

Neither man had moved toward her, but she could see they were tightly sprung coils, ready to pounce if she made any sudden movements.

Erin pulled her T-shirt over her head. She'd shed her bra about thirty seconds after getting home from work, something both her lovers clearly appreciated now.

"Fuck," Gavin whispered reverently, his gaze locked on her breasts. She'd never been with anyone who'd ever made her feel truly beautiful before Gavin and Oliver. It was a heady, wonderful thing, something she wished every woman on the planet could feel at some point in their lives.

Next, she shed her lounge pants, kicking them off. She hadn't bothered with panties either, when she'd come home and changed out of her scrubs. So two discarded pieces of clothing later, she was completely naked.

"Your turn," she said.

Oliver shot Gavin a look when he popped the top button on his flannel. Gavin gave him a grin that screamed "oops," and lowered his hands.

"Um...I'm waiting," she said, perfectly aware she was provoking the beasts.

Oliver's eyes narrowed, his hand fisting on the scarf looped around his palm. "Get on the bed, Erin."

She tilted her head, trying to decide her next move. She loved the idea of a chase, but she was still standing too close to them. If she tried to run now, they'd catch her before she made it to the bedroom door.

Her hesitance didn't go unnoticed by either man.

"Do it now and we'll take it easy on you," Gavin said.

Foolish man. Easy was the last thing she wanted.

"Just your shirts," she asked, feigning an innocence neither man was buying. "Please? I love looking at you."

Oliver and Gavin exchanged a look. While it was clear Oliver was ready to put his foot down, Gavin was still too new to their bedroom play. And too anxious to get to the good stuff. Something she intended to use to her favor.

"Pretty please," she said, directing her request only to Gavin.

Once more, Gavin lifted his hands and unbuttoned another button. Oliver reacted exactly as she anticipated, taking his attention from her to reach out and still Gavin's actions. That split second of distraction was all she needed as she spun around and sprinted toward the door.

She was only halfway down the hall when a strong arm banded her around the middle, pulling her to an abrupt halt.

"Bad girl," Oliver murmured in her ear.

She shivered, not with fear but excitement.

As Oliver dragged her back to the bedroom, she realized Gavin hadn't given chase. When they entered the room, she spotted him standing next to the bed, his shirt completely unbuttoned and hanging open. Likewise, he'd unbuckled his belt, but it still remained in the loops of his jeans. He was the very image of a dangerous bad boy, and she wasn't the only one affected by him.

"Jesus," Oliver murmured, still gripping her tightly.

She wiggled her ass against Oliver's denim-clad erection. He was rock hard, ready to go. But the past year had proven her boyfriend was a master when it came to building a scene. His patience in their sexual play was unshakeable. And God knew she'd tried to shake it a time or three thousand.

"Bring her over here," Gavin directed.

Erin wasn't sure she'd survive if Gavin turned out to be as dominant as Oliver in the bedroom.

She noticed the scarves Oliver had retrieved from the closet on the bed...waiting for her.

Gavin pointed toward the floor. "Kneel there, sweet girl. I think you promised me and Ollie blowjobs."

Erin was on her knees before she could even finish processing the request. She wanted this. Wanted *them*.

Oliver stepped next to Gavin, both of them lowering the zippers on their jeans. Erin reached up, intent on taking them in her hands, but Gavin stopped her, cupping her cheek in his large palm, tipping her head back until she was looking at them.

Oliver grabbed one of the scarves from the bed and made quick work of claiming her hands, tying them behind her back. She tested the knot, though she should have realized Oliver didn't mess around when it came to bondage.

"And now," Gavin said, his voice so low it sounded like a growl, "we get serious."

Oliver watched as Erin shivered in response to Gavin's sensual threat. With her hands tied behind her back, her beautiful, large breasts were pushed out, and he couldn't resist reaching down to pinch one of her hard nipples.

Erin moaned, her eyes drifting closed.

They couldn't have that.

Oliver released her breast and gripped a handful of her hair in his fist, tugging on it until she was looking up at them. Her eyes were cloudy with arousal—their girl had a penchant for hair pulling—and it took everything Oliver had not to toss her face-down on the bed and pound inside that sweet pussy of hers.

However, Gavin clearly had different plans. He might still be new to sex with a woman, but damn if he hadn't taken to it like a fish in water.

"Give me her mouth," Gavin demanded.

Oliver used his grip on her hair to direct her toward Gavin.

"Open up, sweet girl," Gavin murmured, his thumb on her lower lip. Erin's lips parted and Gavin grasped his dick, pushing the head of it inside.

Oliver kept his hand in her hair and he used it now to push her closer. A soft gagging sound told him Gavin's cock was brushing the back of her throat, so he pulled her away a moment before pushing her back.

Gavin groaned, the sound deep and guttural. "Fuck, that feels good." He lifted his gaze to Oliver. "Go faster."

Oliver picked up his pace, pushing and pulling Erin's mouth along their lover's dick. Erin didn't resist, didn't bother to hide how much she loved Oliver's control. Her soft mews, her hard nipples, the way she pressed her thighs tightly together told him everything he needed to know. She was sensual and adventurous, and while she'd kick his ass if he ever actually called her a submissive out loud, there was no denying that—in the bedroom—that was exactly what she was.

"Look at me, Erin," Gavin said, his hand cupping her cheek. "Let me see those pretty brown eyes while you take me in your mouth."

Oliver stood to her side so when she lifted her gaze, Gavin wasn't the only one who got to see the arousal in her eyes.

Oliver used his free hand to touch Gavin, running a hand along his back until it landed on his ass.

Gavin cursed when Oliver ran his finger along his lover's ass crack. They'd only spent two nights as a threesome and their play had been limited to simply sharing Erin, taking turns making love to her.

Tonight, Oliver wanted more. A hell of a lot more.

Leaning closer, he bit Gavin's tattooed shoulder, even as he kept directing Erin forward and back on their lover's dick. She was watching them now, so she wasn't missing anything. Something she proved when she hummed her approval.

"I'm going to fuck your ass tonight," Oliver murmured to Gavin. "Going to fuck you while you fuck our girl."

Gavin jerked and Oliver chuckled, aware he was pushing Gavin to his breaking point when he pushed Erin closer, driving his dick deeper into her mouth.

"She's, Jesus, I'm..." Gavin said, his words fading as his eyes clenched with a pleasure that looked like pain.

"Take him all the way in, Erin," Oliver demanded. "Show him, swallow him down."

He'd taught Erin how to open her throat shortly after they'd started sleeping together. Their woman gave seriously amazing head, something Gavin hadn't experienced yet.

"Goddammit!" Gavin swore through clenched teeth. "If you don't stop, I'm going to come."

"Good."

"Fuck, Ollie," Gavin said. "I want..."

"You want it all. You want to come in our pretty girl's mouth *and* her pussy. And you want me in your ass."

Gavin's hand covered Oliver's in Erin's hair, but Oliver couldn't tell if he was trying to stop him or drive Erin deeper, faster. He was close to coming, that much was obvious.

"Do it," Oliver prodded. "Come in her mouth. She wants it as bad as you do."

Erin hummed her assent, her eyes pleading Gavin for exactly what Oliver was offering.

Whatever tenuous grip Gavin had on his control slipped, and his hips flew forward, moving to take even more. Three thrusts later and he was coming.

Erin swallowed every drop, her gaze shifting from Gavin's face to Oliver's as Gavin called out both of their names.

Oliver had never seen so much love written in another person's expression before, never heard his name spoken with such genuine desire, and he wondered how he'd lived a single minute of his life without these two in it.

Oliver released his grip on her hair, massaging her scalp gently. Neither he nor Gavin had been gentle with her. "Are you okay?" he whispered, suddenly worried they'd gone too far.

Erin grinned. "I want to do that every night."

Oliver chuckled at Erin's desire and the look of pure amazement on Gavin's face. "You wasted a whole year, bro."

Gavin shook his head, and Oliver got the sense his best

friend was still trying to figure out if all of this was real or if he was dreaming. "I'm an idiot," he said at last.

Reaching down, he and Gavin both helped Erin stand, her hands still tied behind her back. Oliver wrapped his arms around her, kissing her as he loosened the scarf, freeing her.

"Think I could convince you guys to lose your clothes?"

"Keep trying to tell us what to do, sweet girl, and I'm going to use one of those scarves as a gag."

"You say that like it's a threat," she joked.

Gavin chuckled. "We're never gonna win. Even with two of us, I think we're outnumbered when it comes to Erin." As he spoke, Gavin shrugged off his shirt and dropped it to the ground before kicking off his jeans as well.

Oliver raised one eyebrow. "Would have thought you'd learned a lesson about going commando."

"Refer back to my previous statement. I'm an idiot. Get undressed, Ollie. I've spent too many years wanting you inside me again. My patience is gone."

Oliver decided there was a time for drawing out the sexual anticipation, taking his time. And then there was tonight. His desires matched Gavin's perfectly.

The first time they'd had sex, it had been amazing, but there had been that missing piece, that one part of the equation that would have made the night perfect.

Glancing at Erin, who was climbing onto the bed, everything fell into place. She crooked her finger at them, and again Gavin proved any restraint on his part was going to be nonexistent the rest of the night.

He crawled over Erin, who parted her legs for him. Resting his upper body weight on his elbows, he kissed her, long and deep and passionately. Oliver shifted to the foot of the bed for a better view. As much as he loved being a part of the kissing, watching was just as hot.

Gavin murmured sweet words as his lips traveled along Erin's soft cheek to her ear. "So beautiful. So fucking beautiful."

Erin lifted her legs, wrapping her ankles around Gavin's waist, her hands tangling in his hair. "Need you," she whispered. "Need you so much."

Gavin's recovery time—considering how hard he'd just come from Erin's blowjob—was impressive to say the least. He shifted until the head of his dick rested at the opening to her body. He pressed in no more than an inch before halting.

"Shit. Condom." He started to pull out, but Erin's legs tightened around him, holding him in place.

"I'm on the Pill."

She and Oliver had done away with condoms a few months into their relationship.

Gavin studied her face for a moment before turning to look at Oliver.

Oliver grinned. "There's nothing like going bareback."

Gavin frowned. "I've never had sex without a condom. Ever."

Erin reached up and turned his face back to her. "It's up to you. I'm just saying—"

Her invitation was cut short when Gavin thrust inside her to the hilt. He took her with a single hard push before he froze, buried deep.

"Holy shit," he whispered. "Holy. Shit." Then he started kissing her again.

Oliver remained where he was for only a minute more. It was all he could manage before his body demanded that he get in on the action. He crossed to the side of the bed and opened the nightstand drawer, retrieving a condom and the tube of lubrication.

Gavin had started thrusting inside Erin, and given the groans and moans from both of them, Oliver realized he was dangerously close to missing the party completely.

He placed one hard slap on Gavin's ass, to draw his lovers' attention. "Stop moving. Wait for me."

Gavin slowed his motions, though the shiver that trembled through his body told Oliver he was struggling to remain still.

"Hurry up," Gavin rasped. "She feels like heaven. I need to—"

Oliver slapped Gavin's ass again. "Wait."

He glanced over his friend's shoulder, catching sight of Erin. Her eyes were closed and it looked like she was in pain as well, poised on the same precipice and ready to take the leap.

"Open your eyes, sweet girl. Watch me."

She lifted heavy eyelids, blinking several times until she could find her focus, find his face.

Gavin shuddered, pushing up from his elbows to his hands, as Oliver squeezed some of the cool lube into his ass. As he worked it in, Oliver realized he wasn't faring much better than Gavin and Erin. He'd never had sex with another man, Gavin his only male lover.

After their first—and only—sexual encounter, Oliver couldn't convince himself that sleeping with another guy wouldn't be cheating. He'd known it was a silly sentiment, given the fact Gavin dated—and had sex with other men—a lot. Of course, Oliver hadn't been living a celibate life, but he'd only taken women to his bed.

He worked one finger in, then two, then three. He was moving too quickly, not taking enough time to prepare Gavin, not that his lover seemed to mind. Each time he added a finger to the game, Gavin thrust into Erin, and it was only Oliver's firm grip on his upper thigh that stopped him from continuing until he came.

Removing his fingers, Oliver pulled on a condom and coated it with lubrication. Then he guided the head of his dick to Gavin's anus.

"It's been so long," he mused aloud.

"Too long," Gavin agreed.

"Please," Erin whispered.

That lone word was the final nail in all their coffins. After that, speech deserted them, the only sounds in the room, those of three lovers drowning in pleasure and desire.

Oliver slid into Gavin's ass, groaning at how tightly it gripped him. Gavin mimicked his slow motion, thrusting into Erin at the same pace. After half a dozen passes, Oliver closed his eyes and gave in to his primal side, slamming in and out of Gavin's ass, his rough thrusts driving Gavin deeper and harder into Erin.

Erin's back arched as she came. If Oliver could have found the breath, he would have chastised her for her lack of control. As it was, it felt as if every speck of air in the room had evaporated as he continued to fuck Gavin's ass, rutting like a wild beast.

Gavin was the next to fall over, his climax sparking another in Erin—or perhaps prolonging her first. Both his lovers cried out loudly, but Oliver couldn't stop, couldn't give way. Not for a goddamn second.

He doubled down, slamming in harder, even as Gavin's strength gave way and he collapsed onto Erin. If she was being crushed, she didn't complain—or even seem to notice.

Oliver thrust in once, twice, three times more before he exploded, splintered into a thousand pieces. Like Gavin, he found it hard to remain upright. He bent over his lovers, resting his forehead on Gavin's slick back.

"Jesus." That one word felt like it was ripped from his chest as he fought for breath.

Neither Erin nor Gavin spoke, and he could hear their gasping breaths as well. Gavin was the first to move, lifting slightly to shrug Oliver off.

"I'm crushing our girl."

Oliver locked his knees and forced himself upright, groaning as his cock slid out of Gavin's ass. He disposed of the condom while Gavin shifted enough to drop down next to Erin before placing a soft kiss on her shoulder.

Erin lay lifeless, her eyes closed as her chest rose and fell.

Oliver claimed her other side, he and Gavin reaching across her, linking hands on her stomach.

"I would ask to do that every single night too, but I think

we'd be dead within a week if we tried it," Erin said, smiling widely even though she was staring at the ceiling. "That was incredible."

"Next time, I'm fucking *your* ass, Ollie."

Oliver grinned, even as he shook his head. "Not so sure about that."

Gavin laughed as Erin patted Oliver's cheek. "Aw. You're so adorable. It would seem you can dish it out, but you can't take it."

Oliver narrowed his eyes and pointed at Gavin's cock. "Have you seen the size of that monster?"

Erin giggled. "You're not exactly a slouch yourself, and Gavin took it like a man."

"That's it," Oliver said, as he sat up and began to tickle her as punishment. Erin squirmed, trying to escape, even as she laughed.

Gavin shook his head at the two of them but didn't join in. "Where the hell do you two find the energy?" he asked. "I can barely move."

"Come on." Oliver stood, then reached down a hand to both of his lovers. They each accepted as he pulled them up. "Let's take a shower together. I'm a sweaty mess."

"A shower sounds good," Erin said.

Gavin groaned, but he still followed them to the bathroom.

Once the water was hot, they climbed in, each jostling for space under the showerhead.

"Think your landlord would lose his shit if I put in a second showerhead on the other side?" Gavin asked.

"Probably," Erin said. "But it would be worth losing my security deposit over."

"Or..." Oliver started, taking the bottle of shampoo from Erin, squeezing a dollop onto his palm, and putting it back on the shelf before twisting her back to him so he could wash her hair. He massaged her scalp as she moaned with pleasure.

"God, that feels good," she said.

"Or?" Gavin prompted.

"Or...we rebuild the apartment above the pub to suit our needs. And we move in there when it's ready."

Gavin grinned. "I like that idea."

"You think your family would care?" Erin asked.

Oliver shook his head. "No. No one wants the apartment. Everyone is happily shacked up in their own places. I love it there," he admitted.

"So do I," Gavin said.

Erin nodded, smiling. "It's awesome and big. We could do some pretty cool things with it."

It was on the tip of Oliver's tongue to point out the space was big enough to raise a family, one with seven kids, but he held back. The last time he'd spouted off his wild dreams, Gavin dug in his heels and walked away. And while he didn't think—God, he hoped—he wouldn't do the same this time, he recalled Gavin telling him all those years ago that he had no interest in bringing a kid into this world.

Oliver prayed he and Erin could change Gavin's mind. Because Oliver didn't just dream wild. He dreamed big.

❧ 14 ❧

Gavin studied his reflection in the mirror and grimaced, debating if he should change. He'd put on a light blue button-up shirt, with a new pair of jeans. Of course, everything he owned these days was new.

For the past week, he and his mother had begun texting daily, and he'd even stopped by the halfway house where she was staying a few times—carefully picking times when he knew she would be at work—to drop things off for her. He'd taken her a new pillow when she mentioned the one in her room was uncomfortable, and he'd loaned her an old hammer when she dropped into the conversation that she'd tripped over a loose floorboard. Two days ago, he'd picked up her prescriptions at her request. He felt slightly guilty because he'd snuck a peek at the medicine bottles and written down the drug names to ask Erin. Apparently his mother was on quite a cocktail of prescription meds, all meant to keep her depression and antisocial disorder under control.

Typically, their texts consisted of little more than quick check-ins. She would ask about his day, he would reply it was fine, and then returned the courtesy of inquiring about hers. Her texts were always longer, including the dropped hints about things she needed. Picking up the prescriptions was the first thing she'd asked him outright to do for her, and he suspected she'd done it as a way of proving she was taking her illness seriously. While he wouldn't say she was exactly happy with her life, she didn't complain as much nowadays as she had when he was younger.

As a kid, he'd grown accustomed to her coming home from work exhausted, dropping down on their threadbare couch, bitching about her aching feet and back and the low tips she'd earned that day. She'd always remained on the couch until bedtime, never moving to pitch in around the apartment, while he brought her dinner and fetched drinks for her.

She'd taken his servitude as her due, treating it as something he owed her, never once thanking him, something he'd never realized was actually a thing until he'd gone to live with the Collinses. His foster parents were forever thanking him for stuff, and he could remember thinking there was something wrong with them when he'd first moved in. He'd actually resented it when they'd said thank-you because he'd thought the words were fake, their attempts at trying to steal him away from his mother.

Sometimes, Gavin struggled to make the boy he'd been match with the man he'd become. It was like he'd changed bodies somewhere along the line, but he couldn't recall when or how.

Yesterday was the first time she mentioned the dinner they'd discussed, texting to see if he would like to get together tonight, claiming that she had a Christmas gift for him. Gavin had been tempted to push her off, to say he was too busy, but he couldn't keep hanging out in this limbo land in terms of his mother.

He'd turned a corner when he'd embraced his place in a relationship with Erin and Oliver, and now it was time to turn another.

Gavin had dropped by Lauren and Chad's office at lunchtime today. He hadn't told any of his foster parents that he'd been in contact with his mom, and given Lauren and Chad's surprise when he told them about his dinner plans for tonight, it was clear Oliver hadn't either.

Not that Gavin would have expected anything different from Oliver. The main reason Oliver had managed to break through his walls was because his foster brother had proven time and time again that he would never betray a confidence, never break a trust.

A few nights after he'd seen Gavin's scars for the first time, Oliver had come into his bedroom and shut the door. Gavin, still not finished fighting, had told him to get the fuck out. Oliver had refused, then he'd made him a vow, promising he'd never tell anyone—their parents included—about the scars. He'd said, "Your stories are yours to tell."

And Oliver had never broken that promise, even when Gavin had hidden how bad the scars were from everyone else. Even when he'd allowed Erin to believe his mother was dead, and now...when his mother had returned to his life.

Lauren and Chad had listened to his concerns and helped him try to put some of his thoughts into perspective. Then they'd done what they'd always done. Told him they'd support him no matter what. Told him they loved him and they were proud of him. Lauren had even called him courageous.

As he looked at his reflection once more, brave was the last thing he felt, and for the millionth time since he'd agreed to this meal, he was tempted to text his mother and cancel.

"Did you fall in?" Oliver called out through the closed bathroom door.

Gavin chuckled even as he took a deep, steadying breath, then stiffened his spine. He didn't doubt for a second he would have already canceled if Oliver and Erin hadn't agreed to go with him.

He opened the door and smiled. His foster brother—no, boyfriend; Gavin decided he liked the sound of that better—had taken some pains with his appearance as well, and he appreciated that Oliver had made an effort despite his anger toward his mom. Oliver, like him, was wearing new jeans, but he'd thrown on a navy-blue sweater instead of a shirt.

Gavin reached out and cupped the back of Oliver's neck, pulling him close for a kiss. He'd meant to keep it quick, platonic even, but that was blown out of the water when Oliver gripped Gavin's belt loops and pulled their crotches together, while opening his mouth to add some tongue action to the kiss.

They parted at the sound of Erin's wolf whistle.

Glancing down the hallway, Gavin felt a bit like whistling himself. Erin spent the majority of her life in either scrubs or yoga pants and T-shirts, so it was rare when they got to see her all dressed up. She'd paired a black sheath with a deep red cashmere cardigan and heels. Her usual ponytail was gone, and the dark hair that betrayed the Italian part of her heritage hung long and loose over her shoulders. She'd put on eyeshadow—something she never wore—and thicker mascara, making her gorgeous brown eyes look even bigger, brighter, more beautiful.

"Jesus," Gavin muttered. Oliver's kiss had gotten him half hard, and now Erin had finished the job. He tried to adjust his suddenly tight jeans to stop them from cutting into his too-erect cock.

"Damn, sweet girl," Oliver said. "How the hell are we supposed to sit next to you in a restaurant and keep our hands to ourselves with you looking like that?"

Erin flushed slightly at their responses. Gavin got a sense she sometimes struggled to accept their compliments as true. Crazy woman seemed to think she was fat, something that drove him nuts. She was curvy in all the right places.

"I don't mind canceling," Gavin said, drawing their attention to his erection.

Oliver punched his upper arm and shook his head. "Nope. We're not letting you back out, so you might as well give your dick the old 'down boy' command right now."

Gavin grimaced. "Easier said than done."

Oliver laughed and pointed to his own crotch. "Tell me about it."

Erin rolled her eyes as she passed between them, continuing down the hallway to the front door. "If we canceled everything on our social calendars based on your hard-ons, we'd never leave the apartment. Let's get this over with so we can come back here and you two can go down on me. I look fucking hot, and I don't want to waste it."

Gavin reached for Erin's coat, helping her put it on, while Oliver, the devil, lifted her skirt slightly and ran his hand over her slit.

"Panties are already damp," Oliver mused aloud.

"Fine," Erin hissed, his light touch obviously making an impact. "It's not just your dicks that would be responsible for our lack of a social life."

Gavin placed his hands on her shoulders and gave her a quick peck on the cheek. "Which is why you're perfect for us."

They hadn't come out to anyone yet about their changed relationship status. Not because they were keeping it a secret, as much as Erin hadn't been lying about their inability to leave the house. Apart from going to work, the three of them were always in too much of a mad dash to hop back into bed together to do much else. Of course, it didn't help that the pub, the place where they'd always hung out the most, was gone. Gavin figured the last few weeks were the longest he'd gone without seeing the countless Collins cousins, aunts and uncles, as well as Pop Pop. He was glad it was almost Christmas so he could reconnect with everyone—particularly Padraig, whom he'd only seen once since the fire.

"Ready?" Erin said, giving him a sweet, comforting smile. Gavin knew she was worried about him and he appreciated her concern.

He nodded. "Yeah." He put on his own jacket, then patted the pocket to make sure the wrapped gift Erin had helped him pick out earlier in the day was there. When his mother had mentioned having a gift for him, he'd sort of felt like he needed to reciprocate. Erin had suggested earrings, then helped him decide on a pair of silver hoops.

The three of them piled into Oliver's pickup truck and they drove to the restaurant. They'd picked a quiet place off the beaten track. It wasn't super fancy, but in Gavin's opinion, they served up some of the best crab cakes in the city.

His mother was already sitting at the table when they arrived, and he tried to swallow down his nervousness and anger when he saw the glass of wine in front of her. They hadn't progressed beyond general niceties, and he hadn't felt comfortable asking about her recovery. It occurred to him—belatedly— he should have had that conversation before they went out together in public.

"Gavin," she said, smiling as they approached the table. Unlike him, she didn't seem to be suffering from anxiety, and he wondered about that. She'd been genuinely nervous at their first meeting, but there was none of that in her now.

She stood up, her arms outstretched for a hug. Gavin didn't feel comfortable embracing her, but refusing would be rude, so he accepted the hug, keeping it quick.

He gestured to his dates. "You remember Oliver and Erin."

His mother nodded, the smile she'd given him fading to something that looked a lot more forced. "Of course I do."

"It's nice to see you again, Ms. Hawke," Erin said, and Gavin could have kissed her for the polite lie. Despite their reservations about his mother and this reunion, neither of them would treat her disrespectfully because they cared about him. They were here to support him, not make things harder.

"Please, call me Cecilia."

Erin nodded, and the four of them sat down before picking up their menus.

"The crab cakes are really good here," Gavin said to his mother.

She shrugged slightly. "Shellfish doesn't agree with me."

Gavin didn't know that. Not that they'd had money to buy fresh fish when he was younger. The majority of their meals came from cans, easy things he could heat up in a pan or microwave.

"The burgers are good too," Oliver offered.

Mom didn't even glance in Oliver's direction or acknowledge that he'd spoken.

"I think I'm going for the salad with grilled chicken," Erin said when the silence shifted into the awkward range. "I've already started to pack on my extra holiday weight and we haven't even gotten to Christmas Day yet."

Gavin chuckled. "You look amazing, Erin. Always."

He felt his mother watching him as he spoke, and he wondered what she was thinking. He'd never brought anyone home with him from school—male or female—because he was never sure which mother was going to be waiting for him. As such, it occurred to him she'd never really seen him in any relationship—friendship or romance—with anyone that wasn't her.

"I thought you might become a chef, Gavin. You were always in our kitchen, cooking something up."

Gavin nodded, swallowing down an uncharitable retort. He cooked because she was always too tired. "I like to eat, so I cook. I wouldn't say it's a passion or anything."

"He's an incredible builder," Oliver said. "You should see this guy on the construction site. Plumbing, electrical work, there's nothing he can't do."

Once again, Mom ignored Oliver.

"You're rebuilding that pub, the place where you lived before the fire?" she asked Gavin.

"Yeah. Well, not me alone. I work for Oliver's uncles and Sean at... Well, we're rebuilding it."

Mom glanced just briefly at Erin before turning her attention back to Gavin. "And you'll move back in there once it's completed?"

While there was nothing wrong with her questions, Gavin

bristled at the idea of sharing any private information with her. He'd even stopped himself from giving her the name of the construction company he worked for.

"That's the plan," Erin answered for him.

Finally, his mother acknowledged someone else at the table besides him. "All three of you?"

Erin was clearly made of sterner stuff than he was. "Yep. Roommates typically live together."

The waiter came to take their orders, and Gavin bit his tongue when his mother ordered another glass of wine.

Once the waiter left, Erin, as always, found a way to fill the silence, telling them all a cute story about one of the interns dressing up as Santa for the kids in the pediatric ward, then launching right into her adventures shopping for a Christmas gift for her grandparents. Erin was blessed with the gift of gab as well as a wicked sense of humor. Gavin was never more grateful for that than now, when he was struggling to think of a single thing to say to his mother.

Mom was quiet, and Gavin wasn't even certain she was listening. Unlike he and Oliver, she didn't ask questions or make comments, and she looked slightly bored.

Gavin focused his attention on Erin and for a little while, he could almost pretend this dinner was like the hundred others he, Erin, and Oliver had shared together over the past year.

The food arrived, providing them a chance to talk about something else mundane and safe. He and Oliver had gone for the crab cakes, Erin the salad, and his mother ordered pasta carbonara, though she ate little of it and instead moved it around on her plate.

"Is it not good?" Gavin asked after a few minutes. "Should we send it back?"

Mom smiled at him, reaching over to place her hand on his. "You always did take such good care of me," she said, as if that answered his question. "Always fretting and worrying about me."

"Would you like to order something else?" he asked, resisting the urge to pull his hand away from hers.

"I got all your packages," she said, ignoring his question again.

"Packages?" Oliver murmured.

This time, there was no denying that his mother was pointedly ignoring Oliver.

"It was so sweet of you to remember me. All those years."

Gavin shrugged, wishing he could think of some way to change the subject.

"What packages?" Erin repeated Oliver's question.

Mom turned her attention to Erin and smiled, though the gesture didn't feel friendly as much as threatening. "Every year I was away, Gavin brought me birthday and Christmas gifts. So thoughtful. Not that I should have been surprised. No matter how many times the state took him away from me, Gavin always fought to get back to me."

He wasn't sure he'd use the word fight. The *state* brought him back. Those words pounded in Gavin's brain, but now, like always, he didn't say them aloud. He considered the foster families he'd been taken to live with, suddenly seeing them with different eyes. He'd always thought them cold, unfeeling people just using the system to get a paycheck. But it occurred to him, a lot of those homes hadn't been bad at all, the foster parents genuinely wanting to help him.

His feelings for them had been driven by his mother. *She'd* been the one to tell him foster parents were bad, that they didn't want him, that no one would ever want him. Then she'd always insist that she was the only person who would ever love him.

He'd lived over half his life believing himself unlovable. Because of her.

What was he doing at this table?

"You took her gifts?" Oliver asked softly.

Gavin swallowed hard and nodded. "Yeah."

"Such a good son," Mom said, though it wasn't clear if she

was responding to Oliver or trying to manipulate him. She leaned close to Gavin once more. "You've always taken care of me. You know...you don't have to rebuild that pub. Maybe you and I..." She let her sentence fade there, the unspoken words hovering in the air.

And that was when he saw it...the slightly unhinged look in her eye, and the slightest smell of whiskey on her breath. She hadn't started with the wine.

This was a mistake. A big fucking mistake.

"I..." Gavin cleared his throat, fighting to say just that, but he couldn't be sure what her response would be. They were in public. And Oliver and Erin were there. He didn't want to subject them to...Jesus...her brand of crazy if this all went south.

"Excuse me a minute, please," Gavin said, rising. "I just need...restroom." As far as quick escapes went, that was probably the worst, but he needed a minute to pull himself together and to figure out how to extract them from the restaurant without making a scene.

Whatever numbness or indecision he'd experienced in regards to his mother had just given way to a barrage of red-hot rage.

He walked to the restroom on wooden legs, then straight to the sink, where he splashed his face with cold water, fighting to calm down. He gave himself just a few minutes, not willing to leave Erin and Oliver alone with his mother for longer than that.

He took a deep breath, releasing it slowly. It didn't help.

Typically he was better at controlling his temper, but tonight...his blood was boiling, his jaw clenched, his shoulders tight. He felt the overwhelming urge to punch the wall.

Dammit.

No. No, he repeated to himself. He wasn't going to give in to the anger, wasn't going to lash out. Wasn't going to be *her*.

He studied his reflection and fought to clear his mind of everything.

Once he'd managed to calm down, he left the restroom.

As he approached their table, he slowed down when he realized his mother was talking, and the outright anger in Oliver's expression gave him reason to pause. Gavin was standing behind her, so she hadn't seen him, didn't realize he was close.

"...don't know what your family did to him, but my son isn't a fag like you. I'm back now, and I'm going to fix him. Even when he lived with you and those freaks you call parents, he never forgot me. Never. Gavin will always come back to me. *Always.* Because I'm the only one he'll ever truly love."

Gavin pulled out a handful of twenties and slapped them on the table next to his mother, causing her to jump in her seat.

"Come on," he said to Oliver and Erin. "We're leaving."

Erin and Oliver didn't hesitate to rise.

"Gavin," Mom said, standing as well. It was apparent she hadn't meant to be overheard. "Wait! Give me a minute to explain. You misunderstood."

He shook his head. "No. I didn't misunderstand a thing. But I'm going to explain some things to *you*, because this explanation is long overdue. You and I no longer have a relationship. Shit, we never had one to begin with. You manipulated, used, and abused me my entire childhood. I'm sorry for what happened to you. I really am. And I know there are some things that are off in your head, so maybe you can't help how you are—but none of that means I have to stand by as a silent victim and take the shit you heap down on me."

"Gavin, please!" Mom was crying, and while he wasn't talking loudly, he could see they were attracting an audience from the nearby tables.

"You want to know what I consider the best night of my life? The night you cut my arm. Because that led me to the Collinses. To Ollie." Gavin glanced at Oliver.

Oliver, his boyfriend, his foster brother, the best friend he'd ever had, gave him an encouraging nod and an understanding smile. "Don't stop now. You've got this."

"Those people," Mom whispered. "The way they live. It's not normal!"

Gavin laughed. "Jesus. Seriously? That's not a good stone for you to throw, Cecilia."

His mother winced as he used her real name. He would never call her Mom ever again.

He had a real mother, Lauren, who loved and supported him. That name was hers from this moment on.

"Gavin. You're all I have," she said through clenched teeth. "You can't leave me."

"Actually..." Gavin stretched out his hand to Erin, who took it and gave it an encouraging squeeze.

"Say it," Erin prodded. "Don't hold back. We're here. We're always going to be here."

She'd stood next to him, offering the same quiet support as Oliver the whole time he'd spoken. Her words gave him the strength he needed.

He turned his attention back to his mother. "I *can* leave you. Because I've found a real family, one who builds me up rather than tearing me down, who supports me, cares for me. And I've got Erin and Ollie and a happy future, a lifetime of love and, God willing, a lot of kids. Kids who will never have to wonder where their next meal is coming from, never have to go to sleep afraid, never know what it feels like to be burned or beaten. I've got a full life now—and there's no room for you in it."

Before his mother could say anything else, Gavin reached out for Oliver, who took his free hand—Erin still clinging to the other—and the three of them walked toward the exit. He could feel the eyes of the restaurant's patrons on them, but he didn't care.

For the first time in his life, he was comfortable in his own skin. He was through with guilt, through with second-guessing everything.

The second they reached the sidewalk, Erin turned toward him, hugging him tightly. "That was awesome."

Oliver tugged Gavin out of Erin's arms to pull him into his. "You were amazing. You *are* amazing." He backed that statement up with a kiss.

"Totally amazing," Erin concurred.

"It's over," Gavin murmured, suddenly feeling empty. After so many years on a roller coaster of pain and emotion, he wasn't sure what to do with the sudden lack of...everything.

"No, it's not. It's just the beginning," Erin said, clasping his hand in hers as she pulled him toward the parking lot. Oliver matched them, step for step.

"So..." Oliver drawled. "Kids, huh?"

That damn goofy grin was back on his best friend's face.

Gavin released his first steady breath since they walked into the restaurant, and rolled his eyes. "You can't just let me have one thing without calling me on it, can you?" he joked. "Fine, Ollie. I was wrong about everything all those years ago. You, me, my sexuality, kids...your wild dreams."

"They aren't dreams anymore," Oliver said, wrapping his arm around Gavin's waist. "We've made them a reality."

Oliver and Gavin kissed quickly as they reached the truck, then they realized Erin had stopped a few feet away from the vehicle.

"Erin."

"I'm all for the reality, but just for the record, I think we're going to need to define what *a lot* of kids looks like."

Oliver and Gavin laughed loudly, neither one offering a response, instead walking back to Erin and dragging her into the truck.

"I mean it," she insisted as Oliver started the truck. "I'm going to need to hear a number."

"Mmmhmmm," Gavin hummed, kissing her deeply.

"You're trying to distract me," she murmured when they parted to suck in some much-needed air.

"Is it working?" Gavin asked.

Erin pouted adorably. "Dammit. Yes."

"Good," he said.

She grasped his hand and lifted it to her breast. "I think you should distract me more."

Oliver groaned and put his foot down on the accelerator. "Wait for me," he insisted.

"Always," Gavin said. "Always."

❧ 15 ❧

Oliver looked around and grinned. Apparently it didn't matter a bit where the Collins clan spent Christmas, it was still going to be fun.

Erin and Layla were two too many cups of eggnog in, giggling loudly with his cousins, Yvonne, Fiona, and Darcy. Gavin was sitting between their dads, Chad and Sean, on the big sectional in Caitlyn's living room, passing around a bottle of Jameson with Padraig, Colm, and Pop Pop as they watched the football game.

The aunts and his mom were busy in the kitchen, mashing the potatoes and preparing the food. The table was always overflowing with platters of turkey and ham, stuffing, at least ten different vegetables, steaming hot rolls with real butter. The aunts would set all the food out so they could help themselves buffet style.

The weather was actually mild enough that they could congregate outside as well as in, this year, despite how cold it had been earlier in the month. Looking through the front window, he saw Aaron chatting with Justin, Killian, and Will on the front porch.

Tomorrow, he, Gavin, and Erin would travel to Philadelphia for another "Christmas" with the Morettis. They also intended to tell her parents about their relationship. Gavin was a little nervous about it, though Erin assured them Layla had paved the way for them in her family as far as committed throuples went. Erin seemed confident her folks would be as understanding as Gavin and Oliver's had been when they'd told them about their changed relationship status last night. They'd gone to his parents' house for Christmas Eve dinner and to open gifts.

"What are you doing standing over here alone?" Gavin said, stepping next to him.

Oliver glanced toward the TV and saw it was halftime. "Just soaking it all in."

Gavin nodded, smiling, then looked around himself. "It *is* pretty awesome."

The family had finished opening their gifts about half an hour earlier, keeping up the tradition of drawing names. This year, the order for opening the gifts had been youngest to oldest —something they'd probably have to continue as more and more of his cousins were having children. By letting the little ones open first, the kids weren't forced to be patient and could play with their new toys while the adults took their time opening gifts.

Plus, Riley had cleverly crafted it so that Pop Pop would be the last to open. Ewan had drawn Pop Pop's name and already given him a brand-new suitcase. They'd been amused to watch Pop Pop ooh and ahh over the thing, even though it was clear he didn't expect to ever really use it.

Little did Pop Pop know...

This year, they'd planned something special, and when he spotted Sunnie pulling all the aunts out of the kitchen, and Colm asking everyone outside to come in, he knew they were about to present it.

Padraig turned off the TV as Tris and Colm joined him in front of it. Everyone had been anticipating this moment, and Oliver watched as the entire family gathered around, jostling for a good spot. When Tris raised his hand, the room fell silent quickly, something Oliver didn't think possible in the Collins family.

Pop Pop looked around the room, his forehead creased in confusion. "What's going on, son?" he asked Tris.

"Pop, would you mind joining us?"

Pop Pop stood up, stepping next to Colm, Tris, and Padraig in front of the big-screen TV. "Should I be worried?" he asked.

Tris chuckled as he shook his head. "No." Then Tris addressed the entire room. "I think we can all agree the last month has been pretty rough for all of us. Losing the pub...and Sunday's Side, as well as our home above..."

Pop Pop nodded as he placed his hand on Tris's shoulder. "It's been a very difficult time indeed."

"So we got together and decided we wanted this year to end on a happy note. There's one last gift for you, Pop. And it's from all of us."

Pop Pop looked around the room. "All of you?"

Padraig pulled an envelope out from behind his back and handed it to their grandfather.

Pop Pop's hands trembled slightly as he opened the envelope. It took a moment before he realized exactly what it was he was holding in his hands. "Plane tickets?"

"Read them," Tris prodded.

Pop Pop's eyes widened. "No. I..." He looked at his son. "Ireland? I'm going to Ireland?"

"*We're* going to Ireland," Tris responded. "You, me, Paddy, and Colm. A guys' trip."

"Just make sure you take in some of the sights, along with your ventures in and out of the pubs," Riley teased. "We want pictures and stories, so take a break from the Guinness every now and then."

"Party pooper," Colm said as everyone laughed.

"You've always wanted to go back, Pop," Teagan said. "But between running the pub and having seven kids, and Mom getting sick, then weddings and grandkids..."

"There was never time or money," Pop Pop said. "But it's too much."

"No, Pop. It's not," Keira said, stepping forward and hugging her dad. "You've given us so much. Please let us give this to you."

"And when you get back...the pub will be ready to reopen," Killian called out.

"It'll all be ready," Sean added. "Sunday's Side. The dorm. We're getting our home back."

Pop Pop gestured toward the suitcase he'd received, sitting next to the couch. "Well, Ewan. I have to admit I wasn't sure I'd ever have a reason to use your fine gift, but it looks like I'll be using it sooner than I expected."

Everyone cheered as Riley and Teagan hugged their dad.

"Wow. What a great gift."

Oliver glanced next to him, smiling at Emmy's observation. "It really is. Look how happy he is."

Emmy watched as Pop Pop slapped Padraig on the back, the two of them laughing. She had first joined them for Christmas last year, when Padraig discovered she'd spent the previous one alone. Emmy's parents were gone and the only other family she had was a brother. But according to Emmy, they'd been estranged for years.

"How long are they going to be in Ireland?" Emmy asked.

"Six weeks," Oliver responded.

"Six weeks," she repeated, still looking at Padraig. "Okay," she murmured sadly.

Oliver wasn't sure what to make of her comment, but as Emmy walked away, joining Sunnie and Yvonne, he worried about the heaviness surrounding the typically cheerful woman.

"What was that about?" Gavin asked quietly.

Oliver shrugged. "No idea."

"Think Padraig will ever figure out how she feels about him?"

Oliver considered that. "I think he knows already, but he won't let himself acknowledge it."

"Yeah. You're probably right. It's a shame because Emmy is perfect for him."

Oliver grinned. "I seem to recall a couple people being perfect for you too, but you took your damn time figuring it out."

Gavin chuckled. "Touché."

Oliver turned around when he felt someone tapping his shoulder. Erin was smiling at him and Gavin as she crooked her finger at them.

They followed her down the hallway, laughing when she pulled them both into the bathroom with her.

The second Gavin closed and locked the door behind them, she was in Oliver's arms, kissing him as if she hadn't seen him in years.

"What's that for?" Oliver asked as they parted.

"Who cares what it's for?" Gavin asked. "Where's mine?"

He tugged Erin away, stealing his own kisses.

"I missed you," she said in between kisses. "And eggnog makes me horny."

"Good information to have," Oliver joked. "That's going to become a weekly staple on our grocery list, right next to butter and milk."

"This is the best Christmas I've ever had," she said.

Gavin nodded. "Same for me."

Oliver shifted closer, the three of them wrapping their arms around each other. "I love you," he murmured, kissing Gavin, then Erin again.

"Think we have time for a quickie?" Gavin asked.

Oliver laughed. Since walking away from his mother at dinner a few nights earlier, Gavin suddenly seemed like a different man, and Oliver realized he'd never understood just how much the past weighed his boyfriend down until Gavin finally shook it off, once and for all.

Gavin was happier, freer, laughing often, finding joy in the little things. Erin had noticed the same thing, remarking on it this morning after breakfast.

"I think Caitlyn would kill us if we had sex in her bathroom," Oliver said.

Erin shrugged. "I bet she and Lucas have already christened this room. And every other one in the house. That man is determined to get his wife pregnant again."

They heard voices down the hall, and Gavin sighed. "Okay. No quickie. But I want a reward for showing so much restraint."

"What did you have in mind?" Oliver asked.

"Holiday role-playing when we get home tonight. I'm going to be Santa, and Erin is going to sit on my lap, whispering all the things she wants for Christmas, even though she's been a naughty girl."

"Sounds pretty PG," Erin said.

"Oh, did I forget to say we're going to be naked and I'm going to be inside you?"

"Do I get a role?" Oliver asked.

Gavin grinned. "You're going to be my elf, feeding me your candy cane."

"Shit." Oliver adjusted his jeans, trying to relieve the pressure on his sudden erection. "How am I supposed to go back out there with a hard-on?"

Gavin ran his hand over the front of Oliver's pants, applying pressure. Then he grasped Oliver's hand and pushed it against his own erection, letting him know he wasn't alone.

"Think anyone would miss us if we snuck out the back door right now?" Erin asked, her flushed cheeks proving she was in a similar state.

Oliver shook his head. "We only get the reward if we show restraint. Besides, I like the idea of spending the next few hours fantasizing about ways to spice up that role-play."

"As long as my reward for restraint is restraint, I'll be good," Erin joked. "Merry Kinkmas to us."

EPILOGUE

"There are my boys," Mom said, inserting herself between Oliver and Gavin shortly before Christmas dinner, wrapping her arms around them. "We're going to eat soon." She gave them both a squeeze. "I'm so darn happy for the two of you."

Oliver laughed, since Mom had said the same thing at least twenty times today.

"Did you tell Pop yet?" she asked.

"Not yet, but we will." He glanced at Erin and realized they'd better do it soon, or she'd be too deep in the eggnog to remember the conversation. After the three of them snuck out of the bathroom, Layla had dragged her off to hear some crazy story Bubbles was telling about her new boyfriend that had most of his cousins in stitches.

"I suspect he won't be surprised. I swear that man has a sixth sense when it comes to romance," Mom said, turning to Gavin, her expression shifting to one of concern.

When they told their parents about their relationship with Erin, they'd also shared the details of their dinner with Gavin's mom.

"You sure you're doing okay?" she asked Gavin.

Gavin leaned down and gave her an affectionate kiss on the cheek. "I'm doing just fine...Mom."

Mom froze, and Oliver got a sense she was trying to figure out if she'd heard Gavin correctly. Then she smiled. "Wow, I love the sound of that."

"Sound of what?"

Oliver saw that both his dads had made their way over to them.

"Gavin just called me mom."

Dad—Chad—laughed as he hugged Mom, who wiped away the happy tears in her eyes. "Jesus. There will be no living with her now."

His other dad, Sean, slapped Gavin on the back. "It's about damn time. Now where's my new name?"

Gavin rolled his eyes. "Do we seriously have to make a big deal about this...Dad?"

"Of course we do. It's the Collins' way. And considering you've been one of us for nine years, I think it's time you start to conform to the craziness," Dad—Sean—joked.

Gavin gave him a salute. "So noted."

"This looks like a fun conversation," Pop Pop said. "Mind if I join in?"

"The boys have some news, Pop," Mom said. She gave him and Gavin both a kiss on the cheek. "I'm going to go help in the kitchen."

She and their dads moved away, giving them privacy to talk to Pop Pop, who was still beaming over his gift from the family. He showed them both the tickets.

"You think Ireland is ready for four Collins men?" Oliver asked.

"Well, ready or not, we're going. I can't wait to show the boys where I grew up, my old stomping grounds." Pop Pop shook his head as if he simply couldn't believe it. "I never thought...well...it will be a wonderful adventure."

Oliver looked for Erin, who was doing some sort of shimmy

dance move with Colm's wife, Kelli, even though there was no music playing.

Yep. It was already too late to include her in this.

"So. You have news?" Pop Pop asked, all ears. The old guy was a sucker for gossip.

Oliver moved closer to Gavin and wrapped his arm around his waist. "Gavin, Erin, and I are dating. We were hoping...well, we'd like to move into the apartment above the pub once it's rebuilt. Feels like a good place to raise a family someday."

Pop Pop's eyes lit up, and Oliver could see the sheen of happy tears. "Well, that is good news indeed. I've always hoped someone would want to live in the apartment, raise their family there, like Sunday and I, but then...after the fire..."

"We're going to rebuild it all, remember?" Gavin reassured him.

Pop Pop placed his hand on Gavin's shoulder. "I know you are, lad. And I can't wait to see it." Then he turned and spotted Erin across the room. She, Bubbles, and Kelli had shanghaied Riley from the kitchen, the four of them playing with the Hula-Hoop Lochlan's adopted daughter, Chloe, had gotten for Christmas. Erin was surprisingly good.

Pop Pop chuckled. "Looks like your girl fits in with the family just fine. And I'm pleased you found yourselves an Irish lass."

"She's only half Irish. And sometimes I think the Italian side is more dominant," Oliver joked.

"Och. Irish will always win out," Pop Pop insisted. "Did I ever tell you what the name Erin means, Ollie?"

Oliver shook his head, grinning. "Nope."

"It means peace."

Oliver's eyes widened. "Same as my name."

Pop Pop nodded. "I think it's safe to say you've both brought peace to each other. And to this fine young man," he added, looking at Gavin.

"They have," Gavin agreed. "Not sure where I'd be right now without either one of them."

"What's Gavin's name mean?" Oliver asked.

"Oh well, his is a fine name. Did you know it comes from the name Gawain?"

Gavin tilted his head. "I didn't know that. Wasn't he a Knight of the Round Table?"

"Yes, he was. Gawain was known to be a fierce and courageous warrior but also compassionate."

Oliver grinned. "That sounds about right."

Gavin rolled his eyes, but it was obvious he was pleased by the description.

"However, there's another meaning that I think I might like better," Pop Pop said.

"Better than elf army?" Oliver joked. "Because I think that one's pretty hard to beat."

He and Pop Pop had been building on their elf army stories since Oliver was just a kid, their made-up tales epic. Erin had once suggested they write them down, claiming they'd make great children's stories.

"Well, I'll let you decide that," Pop Pop said. "Gavin also means white hawk."

"No. No way!" Gavin said, shocked. "There's no way my mom knew that."

Oliver agreed. "That's a crazy coincidence." Then he laughed. "So basically your name is White Hawk Hawke."

"Why do I get the feeling you're going to have a lot of fun with that fact?" Gavin asked.

Oliver wiggled his eyebrows. "Because you know me well. And it's perfect timing, because I'd just reached the tail end of the butt jokes."

"Asshole," Gavin muttered good-naturedly.

"Or maybe not," Oliver teased.

"Boys," Pop Pop said, amused by their interplay. "You know,

the Native Americans believed that seeing a white hawk meant a miracle was on the way."

"Now that's more like it." Gavin shoulder-bumped Oliver. "Hear that, Ollie? I'm a miracle. Pretty sure that trumps your silly little elves."

"Damn," Oliver was forced to admit. "I think it does."

"Hey," Erin said as she approached them. "Your mom sent me over. Said we're about to start eating."

Pop Pop reached out and took Erin's hands, giving her a kiss on the cheek. "The boys just told me your good news."

"What? Without me?" she asked.

"Didn't want to interrupt your Hula-Hooping," Oliver joked.

Erin laughed. "Did you see my mad skills?"

Gavin wrapped his arm around her waist. "We saw."

"Very impressive," Oliver said, playfully tugging on her hair.

Pop Pop grinned at the three of them. "Well, I'll leave you three alone. I see Will, Lochlan, and Lucas hovering near the table. If I get in line behind those three vultures, there won't be any of Riley's crab dip left for me."

They laughed as Pop Pop crossed the room and pointedly cut in front of the other men, who all loudly protested. Riley's crab dip was always the most sought-after, and had been the root of more than a few good-natured Christmas arguments whenever someone missed out on getting some.

"I love your family," Erin said, smiling widely.

"And they love you." Oliver gave her a kiss.

"And *we* love you," Gavin added, stealing his own kiss from Erin before giving Oliver one as well.

Oliver caught sight of more than a few family members glancing in their direction, with Finn and Miguel high-fiving as Padraig gave him a thumbs-up.

He chuckled. "Well, that's one way to tell our entire family about us."

Gavin looked around and realized what they'd just revealed. "Oops," he joked, though he obviously didn't mind who knew about them. Hell, Oliver would be surprised if Gavin didn't put a billboard up announcing it soon.

Erin noticed they'd drawn an audience as well and giggled when Sunnie mouthed, "Details now," as Darcy waved her over.

"I've been summoned," she said, giving them both another quick kiss before crossing the room for her fifth degree from his cousins. Not that Erin seemed to mind the questions at all.

"You're really finished fighting it, aren't you?" Oliver asked Gavin. "You've accepted that this is your family, that you belong here."

Gavin nodded, wrapping his arm around Oliver's shoulders. "Yeah. I have."

"Took you long enough," Oliver teased, giving Gavin a quick kiss. "And, bro...welcome to the wild side."

Don't miss out on Padraig's second chance at happily ever after, Wild Chance is coming August 2021. You can preorder it now!

And be sure to join Mari's newsletter to receive a **FREE** sexy Wilder Irish novella, One Wild Night.

Have you read the entire Wilder Irish series? All the books are standalone, so they can be read in any order. Be sure to check out all of them!

Wild Passion
Wild Desire
Wild Devotion
Wild at Heart
Wild Temptation
Wild Kisses
Wild Fire

Wild Spirit
Wild Side
Wild Night
Wild Embrace
Wild Dreams
Wild Chance

Fans of Wild Irish AND Facebook! There's a group for you. Come join the Wild Irish Facebook group for sneak peaks, cover reveals, contests and more! Join now.

WILD CHANCE

It's been three years since Padraig Collins lost the love of his life, Mia, and since then, he's been sleepwalking his way through each day, focusing only on work and family, while hanging out with his best friend, Emmy. He's determined to make that enough, not ready or willing to take a chance on loving and losing again.

The sum equivalent of Emmy's experience with relationships is contained within the pages of the romance novels she writes while sitting at the end of the bar at Pat's Pub. That is if she doesn't count the secret crush she's been harboring for Padraig since the first day she laid eyes on him. Unfortunately for her, Paddy's heart still belongs to Mia.

One tragedy later, Padraig finds himself reaching out to Emmy, only to discover she's no longer there. And it will take the combined romantic efforts of the entire Collins' family to help him win the heart of his best friend...and his second chance at happily ever after.

Preorder Wild Chance now.

ABOUT THE AUTHOR

Virginia native Mari Carr is a New York Times and USA TODAY bestseller of contemporary romance novels. With over two million copies of her books sold, Mari was the winner of the Romance Writers of America's Passionate Plume award for her novella, Erotic Research. She has over a hundred published works, including her popular Wild Irish and Compass books, along with the Trinity Masters/Masters Admiralty series she writes with Lila Dubois.

Find Mari Carr on the web at
www.maricarr.com
mari@maricarr.com